RAVAGERS

C.A. GLEASON

ISBN: 1984193090
ISBN 13: 9781984193094

Cover art by Darko Tomic

Part 1

The Dark Mountains

Chapter 1

Planet Tuhrelevim. 93 percent uncharted. Integration of acclimatized human population delayed.

⅄

At Fort Beckett, Captain Nev was on his weekend run. He ran alone and always at 5:00 a.m. sharp, to stay tip-top. This was in addition to running with his platoon Monday through Friday. His route was four times around the inside of the base, equivalent to roughly six miles.

A soldier on CQ duty emerged from the headquarters building and yelled to Nev as he passed, but Nev didn't hear him. The track vehicles were rolling past; the mechanics were working through the weekend again. The soldier slung his weapon and ran after him.

"Captain Nev!"

Nev turned and jogged in place.

"Orders, sir," he said, handing over an envelope. "Good day, sir."

"Good day, soldier."

The soldier had accomplished his mission and range walked back to his post.

Nev decided to end his run and walk it out. He only had a lap left anyway. He felt sweat trickle down his head as he ripped open the envelope.

⅄

Nev stood at the front of the briefing room doing roll call, mentally evaluating his soldiers.

"Sergeant Brutton."

"Here, sir."

Brutton was short and stocky, so much so that he'd been nicknamed "Bowling Ball" by his teammates on his high-school football team.

"Staff Sergeant Clark."

"Sir."

The squad's section chief was the kind of skinny that a belt hardly helped. Nev knew him when he first came in. He'd been ordered to eat more, and he did, but it didn't help. His metabolism was just too fast.

"FNG."

"Here, sir!" Grady said.

The squad laughed at his enthusiasm. Grady had joined the military when he was older than most. When he began his military career, he didn't have the energy that the younger soldiers had, and he'd been razzed about his lack of motivation.

"RTO."

"Here, sir," Jenkins said.

When a safety briefing was given before a weekend—no fighting, drugs, or anything else that would get a soldier in trouble—it was meant for soldiers like Private First Class Jenkins. He just liked to fight. His nose had been broken at a bar his first week at permanent party, and he never got it fixed.

"Staff Sergeant Lagler."

"Sir."

Lagler was one of the most focused and motivated soldiers Nev had ever had the pleasure of serving with. It was why he was in charge of the armory.

"Specialist McRae."

"Should I stand, sir?"

The others laughed. McRae's six-foot, six-inch frame loomed over the other troops even while sitting.

"Shut up, Specialist. Where's my medic at?"

"Sir," O'Meara said.

Specialist O'Meara lifted weights any chance he got, usually with Brutton, and his uniforms barely fit him.

"What have you done to yourself?" McRae said.

O'Meara smirked. "Don't hate."

Nev folded his hands behind his back. "Any questions?"

Grady raised his hand. "Do we get cooks on this one, sir?"

"Do we ever? MREs, you get first pick, Private."

"Any other good news, sir?" Clark said.

"No smoking on this one."

Groans.

"Bring the alternatives if you need to and use litter discipline."

Grady pantomimed smoking a cigarette. "I'm going to smoke about a pack tonight."

"I'll be laughing at you on our next run," Jenkins said.

Nev went to the position of attention. "On your feet!"

The rest of the soldiers stood and snapped to attention as Colonel Horne entered.

"As you were, gentlemen," Horne bellowed.

The men sat down again, and Captain Nev joined them.

Horne marched to the front of the room and turned toward the men. He was tall, barrel chested, and had a commanding voice, probably even while ordering coffee. "Men, you've read your orders."

Nev knew some of the missing soldiers. "Sir, anything we should know about the previous mission that would assist us in locating them?"

"Unfortunately, their mission and yours are classified. We've speculated there may be similarities to the Ontarian situation, but we aren't certain."

"What was their location before contact was lost?"

"Roughly fifteen hundred klicks."

"That's over nine hundred miles," Grady whispered.

"No shit," Jenkins whispered back.

Nev turned to Clark, and Clark made a half turn, giving an annoyed look. Grady's and Jenkins's military bearing returned.

"How many probes have been sent?" Nev said.

"Hundreds," Horne said. "None have been able to send back data."

"Any idea why?"

"We aren't sure. This planet is as foreign to us as Earth's oceans in the twentieth century. My guess is the weather. That's where you come in. After you assess the location, send a transmission. I'll send more probes. Hopefully they'll make it through."

"Anything else required from the mission, sir?"

"Other than searching for survivors, no."

The door behind Horne opened, and a sinewy man with glasses came into the room. He had blond hair that was nearly white, and he was wearing a jumpsuit.

"This is Doctor Nimbus, biologist. He's helped us on previous missions. He knows this planet better than anyone. Knows the geography and the wildlife. He'll be assisting you in any way he can. We've paid him enough for that."

Nimbus smiled.

"Putting the mission aside, the territory you're going to is like nothing you've ever seen. Beautiful. Like Earth, so I've been told. Good luck."

⅄

Later outside, the squad smoked and joked. Nev focused on the aircraft behind the pilots, Chief Warrant Officers Miller and Gilroy.

"It's an Adelpa," Gilroy said.

"Adelpa two," Nev said, looking the aircraft over.

Gilroy smiled. Adelpa 2s were perfect for low-altitude travel. Nev had never flown in one; he'd only been flown into battle on the Adelpa 1, but he knew that they were lightweight and spryly maneuverable, yet they could fly a decent amount of cargo.

Nev saw the men were antsy; the smokers had snuffed their butts. "Weapons brief. Let's go."

Chapter 2

A waist-high stone wall separated the firing area from the range, and a large case was located in the corner.

"Men, prepare to be impressed," Nev said.

He raised the top of the case to reveal two pod-shaped cannons. Beside them were two controls that each had a stock, handle, trigger, and a digital sight lens but no barrel.

"Is that what I think it is?" Lagler said.

"Patience, Sergeant."

Nev hefted one of the cannons out of the case and laid it on the floor. He retrieved the control and flipped a switch down with his thumb, which activated it. The cannon immediately jolted to life and rose, hovering over Nev's right shoulder.

"This is the M-three-three-one-A-two weapon system, a.k.a. the Shoulder Devil. Sixty-three pounds on its own, two thousand five hundred sixty-three pounds fully loaded."

"Damn," Grady said.

"Don't let it fall on your toe."

The men laughed.

"Looks like it belongs on a tank. We all get one?" McRae said.

"You wish," Nev said. "Just these two. Standard Rovla assault rifles for everybody as usual."

McRae made a disgusted sound.

"Why the big guns, sir?" Grady said.

"Apparently required for where we're going—possibility of animal attacks. Previous missions reported seeing something watching them from a distance. Anyway, it has a magnetic levitation system to handle its weight and recoil. Wherever you aim the control, it targets with surgical precision. Also works for you lefties, Clark."

Nev passed the controller over to Clark, who held it with his left hand, and the SD moved over his left shoulder.

"Obviously you fire it by pulling the trigger. There's a three-second delay to seat the twenty-millimeter rounds before firing. Ammo is stacked and packed in the Devil itself."

Clark passed it to O'Meara.

"What's its capacity?" O'Meara said.

"Ten thousand rounds."

"What about its rate of fire, sir?" Jenkins said.

"Five thousand rounds a minute. It's not without its bugs, though. You'll hear it stutter if the rounds have to seat again, leaving the controller at risk, a glitch still present from the experimental model. Side arms are recommended in a pinch."

Lagler held out his hand, and O'Meara passed the SD controller to him. "Heard about 'em, but never held one." Lagler examined it. Then he looked up behind him and raised and lowered the controller. The SD mimicked his movements perfectly. "Will you tell us about distant targeting, sir?"

"Distant targets aren't a problem because the Shoulder Devil will ascend to the appropriate height and can even be deployed to hunt down and kill each target."

"How high will it go?" Lagler said.

"Sixty meters, approximately. Height targeting dramatically increases ballistics capability, which means you could put rounds on a target from miles away if it can be tagged accurately. Multiple targets can be tagged within the scope, which registers in the Devil's computer, and if you don't want to deploy them, you can tag targets to reach a certain distance before they're fired upon for maximum destructive capability."

"Holy shit. What if they don't reach that distance?" Lagler said.

"Then they won't fire," Nev said.

"Can I see it?" Brutton said.

Lagler passed the controller to him. "What about reloading?"

"It travels to the automated ammo box when commanded, reloads, and comes back."

"How do they coordinate when both are fired at once?" Lagler said.

"They're independent, but their data is linked. Targets that are tagged register with both weapon systems. No duplicates. You can fight a war on your own."

"How loud are they?" Jenkins said.

"Loud. Earplugs are mandatory, and the Shoulder Devils are for emergencies only. Right, Nimbus?"

Nimbus looked bored. "I've never seen them fire."

"You have, though, haven't you, sir?" Lagler said.

Nev took the controller back from Brutton. "Yes, one of the first models."

Chapter 3

Nev sat on his porch with his wife Kate. The sun had already gone down, and both had finished a substantial amount of wine.

"Quick, huh? Back before I know it?" Kate said.

"That's the plan. We don't have much responsibility."

"It's military responsibility, though."

He knew what she was getting at. To Kate, every mission was dangerous, which was technically accurate, especially since the groundwork for colonization of the planet had just begun. She'd been around the military long enough to know how things were.

Except that there were missions that made Nev nervous and ones that didn't. He tended to exaggerate the danger of the safe ones and be close-lipped about the missions that were dangerous. She hadn't caught on so far. Only, she seemed to be keen on this one. Bottom line was he just didn't want his wife to worry about him.

"A civilian could do our job."

"Then why don't they?" she said.

Nev looked away from her, engaged by the mountains in the distance as the summer bugs flew about.

"Huh, why don't they?"

Nev laughed. "I heard you. There aren't that many of us here yet." He sucked the last drop of wine out of his glass. "More wine?"

Kate held her glass out, meeting his gaze. Nev grabbed both glasses and went inside.

He came out with them both full and handed one to his wife. He sat down and took a sip. "I say we head inside after this glass. What do you think?"

Kate studied him. He only wanted to enjoy her company before he left. Not worry or upset her. She understood.

"OK," she said and chugged the entire glass.

Nev did the same. Then he offered his hand, which she gladly took in hers, and they went inside.

Chapter 4

As the men boarded the Adelpa 2, Lagler remote-controlled a minimobile, a six-wheeled five-meter-long weapon-transport vehicle. It held spare weapons, ammo, and tools in its bottom compartments.

Lagler applied the brake halfway up the ramp, and Brutton and O'Meara hefted four automated ammo boxes for the SDs on top and strapped them down.

Nev yanked on the straps. "Go ahead."

Lagler drove the minimobile the rest of the way inside, and after Brutton and O'Meara boarded, Nev did too.

The aircraft lifted off. Miller and Gilroy piloted the craft. The rest of the soldiers sat strapped in on both sides of the interior.

Captain Nev stood, wobbly, at the front of the craft. He pointed to a holographic map with a pointer. "This is the LZ. We'll pick up this trail and hopefully find them within this two-mile radius," he said and circled the point on the map twice. "Catch some z's if you need them."

As the Adelpa 2 skimmed across the planet surface, small mountains were soon dwarfed by larger ones that appeared behind them through soft white mist.

The planet teemed with forest growth, a lot more than evident from their view from the base. Blues and greens hued the atmosphere.

A large lake appeared. It reached across the landscape, stretching between two mountains. The Adelpa 2 gracefully landed in front of an eighteen-meter

Cryton boat that sat in the water, tied to a dock buoy. The platform lowered, and the men filed out.

"We take the boat to the complex," Nimbus said.

"What complex?" Brutton said.

Nimbus pointed into the mist. "That way."

Lagler drove the minimobile out of the Adelpa 2.

"Why can't we land there?" Jenkins said.

"The lake makes the soil too soft," Nimbus said.

"So where are the animals at, biologist?" Grady said.

Nimbus pointed up. A flock of silent flying creatures covered the sky. They had long upturned snouts, and a strange texture covered their bodies, featherlike but not exactly, more like muddy fur.

A dozen spherical probes rocketed past overhead, and the flying creatures swarmed. The soldiers watched as the flying creatures attacked each probe, destroying them.

"There's your answer, Captain," Nimbus said. He took pictures of the creatures.

McRae walked up to Nimbus. He pointed through the valley, where there were dark mountains far in the distance. "How's the fishing?"

Nimbus acknowledged the joke and smiled. He didn't address Specialist McRae though, as if he were beneath him. He aimed his response at Nev instead, which sent looks between the men.

"Our scanners have found most of this planet's life to be there," he said. "They stay there. The animals here are extremely territorial. Needless to say, we won't be going there for a long time."

Lagler drove the minimobile up a ramp onto the boat. A seat rounded the length of it on both sides. Miller climbed to the captain's perch on the second floor and started the engine. The boat accelerated quickly.

"He always gets to drive," Clark said.

The soldiers laughed, but Nimbus didn't, as if he were growing tired of all the comments.

"Why was a complex built here?" Nev said.

Nimbus forced a smile. "You tell me, Captain."

"Something's down there," Clark said.

Nev turned around and looked into the water. Shapes moved. They came closer to the surface. Water creatures. They could be seen clearly now.

"There are shock prods in that drawer there," Nimbus said and motioned casually. "In case they get too close. Captain, will you instruct one of your men to retrieve them?"

"Lagler," Nev said.

Lagler walked to the base of the operating column, opened the drawer, and passed the shock prods around.

Without warning, the creatures leapt out of the water and attached themselves all over the boat, startling everyone except Nimbus. Most of the soldiers got up and took a step back. They were about the size of a medium-sized dog, and like them, they had four legs.

"Are they dangerous?" Nev said.

Nimbus shrugged. He got close and took a photo.

Nev examined the creature a few feet from him, and it seemed to inspect him just as curiously. It looked ferocious. Small fins lined its forest-green body and face, and a patch of even larger knife-shaped fins protruded from its back. Its eyes were sunken into the side of its head, and its top and bottom teeth overlapped its lips.

There was a dark patch ahead of the boat, and it was getting closer.

"It's a school of fish," Nimbus said. "They're attracted to the boat. These ones like to surprise their prey."

When the school was close enough, all the creatures leapt off the boat and dove into the center of it. The school erupted into singles, swimming for their lives. Hunter and hunted swam toward the valley. Then they were gone.

"When were you here before?" Nev said.

"For a few weeks right after the complex was finished," Nimbus said as he examined his most recent photo in the camera's view screen.

"What was your mission?"

"Missions are for soldiers. I'm a contractor."

"Habit. Been in too long."

"Please, Captain, any questions you may have, address me once we've settled in."

Chapter 5

The boat slowed into another dock buoy. Gilroy jumped onto the dock and tied the boat securely.

Nev commanded his squad to unload the boat and then helped out too, never being one to stand idly by as work was being done. Each soldier grabbed his gear, armor, and weapons. Lagler drove the minimobile off the boat, and the soldiers made their way up a short hill.

The land before them flattened out for about a hundred meters, and small hills surrounded the path. The miniature valley led to a perfectly square three-story-high complex.

Nev pushed the code into the digital console located next to the door, and it buzzed open. They all went in, except for Lagler, who drove the minimobile into the garage on the side of the complex.

A wide hallway ran right and left. Stairs accessed each floor at one end, and an elevator accessed each floor at the other. Nev asked Nimbus to take them on a tour so they could familiarize themselves with the layout.

The top floor was a series of offices and rooms for storage, and it ended in stairs that accessed the roof. The barracks and mess hall were on the second floor. The operations center and armory were on the first floor, and there was a door that led to the garage.

The armory's back stock of weapons and ammo were adequate but not ideal. Clearly, they were only for if the shit hit the fan.

"We bringing the Devils, sir?" Grady said.

"No, Private," Nev said. "First phase of our mission is recon only."

"Really?"

"I take orders, same as you." Nev could see Grady still wasn't buying it. "They don't want to jeopardize the tech."

Grady nodded.

As the soldiers geared up, Nimbus approached Nev. "I'm coming with you."

Nev tightened his armor. "We need you here."

"Captain Nev, this is the perfect opportunity for me to—"

Nev held up a hand. "I understand, but you aren't mission essential, and you're a potential liability."

Clark laughed to himself.

"We'll scout the location first. If I feel that you're needed, you'll join us on the next outing."

"Colonel Horne sent me."

"Colonel Horne put me in charge of this mission. You were sent as an advisor. If I need your advice, I'll ask for it. Right now I don't need it." Nev put a hand on his shoulder and looked him right in the eye. "No need to endanger lives unnecessarily."

Nimbus gave a slight, reluctant nod.

"Stay here and assist my RTO, Private Jenkins, in any way possible please."

"All right."

Chapter 6

The *Adelpa 2* flew close to the planet's picturesque landscape. The sun shined radiantly, penetrating the windshield and throwing an orange glow throughout the aircraft.

"Sir, we have an indication of a breadcrumb trail," Miller said.

Blips waved on the radar.

"Lock and load," Nev ordered the men.

The soldiers pulled the charging handles on their automatic Rovla assault rifles.

The Adelpa 2 landed, and the soldiers emerged dressed in full battle rattle, except for Gilroy, who was staying with the aircraft. Colossal blue craggy mountains tipped with white snow enveloped the distance.

"Keep an eye out for any indication to where the missing in action may be, no matter how insignificant, and report anything to me, got it?" Nev said.

"Yes, sir!" the men said.

"Captain, were you picked for this mission because of the Ontarian situation?" Lagler said. "The rumors of animal attacks?"

"One of the reasons, I suppose."

"What was the Ontarian situation?" Grady said.

"Captain here was stranded on a dead station on the outer rim of Syklibus. A horde of space bugs attacked them. Captain blew them all away. He was found among a hundred carcasses."

"They weren't that tough," Nev said. "Just had sharp teeth."

"I hate bugs. That must have been a blast, huh, Cap?" McRae said.

"No. I lost twelve men. Almost lost my leg."

McRae spat on the ground. "Fucking bugs."

"They were just defending what was theirs."

⅄

Nimbus downloaded pictures into his laptop. He was focused, entranced even. Each new species was categorized, and there was a folder for adding data to the established species. The amount was substantial, nearly a hundred.

Nimbus leaned back and stretched. He'd been at it for a while, as long as Nev had been on the mission. He looked over at Jenkins, who was reading a magazine and had the mic and cord draped over his neck, ready to answer any communication from Nev.

"Doing all right?" Jenkins said.

Nimbus nodded. "Fine."

"You look tired."

"Just stretching is all."

Jenkins nodded. "What are you working on?"

"Something above your pay grade," Nimbus said, and he returned to his work.

Jenkins glared at Nimbus before going back to his magazine.

Every time Nimbus closed a file, it was automatically uploaded and sent to Horne. He had instructed Nimbus that he was the only addressee privy to what he discovered.

Chapter 7

Clark spotted the first breadcrumb, a marker flag that was embedded in the ground. It aligned with the next marker and blinked from its beacon, creating a trail to follow. Cheaper than GPS. Typical military.

"See it, sir?" Clark said.

"I see it," Nev said.

All saw that the breadcrumbs were leading between mountains.

The ground abruptly turned from a lush grass to scorched crust, almost like a desert.

"Climate change?" Lagler said.

O'Meara scanned the distance. "Looks like it's just here, though."

"It's an impact site," Nev said.

The men looked at Nev. He was right. The area looked like it had taken a barrage of ordnance.

"We're close," he said.

A thick morning fog rolled up, making it difficult to see. The men were almost between the small mountains when O'Meara saw something. He picked up a bullet casing. "Sir."

"Halt," Nev said.

The men stopped. Casings were everywhere. Grady, McRae, and Brutton kicked at the dirt, exposing even more. Lagler picked up a handful.

A few hundred meters away, slightly past the mountain on their right, was a large growth of grass at least ten feet tall. A grass forest. Shell casings sparkled all the way to it.

"They were either trying to get in that grass or get away," McRae said.

"You can't tell from up there?" Grady said.

McRae grinned. "Funny."

"Get away. The casings point toward it," Nev said.

"I wonder where we're going," Grady said.

Lagler clapped him on the back. "Just think about your savings account."

The men moved in front of the grass forest, waiting for an order from their captain, when a deep grumble came from the grass.

"What is that?" Brutton said.

"Sounded like a growl," Clark said.

Brutton made a move forward, but Nev stopped him short with a powerful arm. "Stay here." Nev inched forward, trying his best to see, to peer into the swirling grass.

The ground suddenly shook, as if hundreds of horses had galloped and shifted their position. Then stillness, just the wind.

"Back up," Nev said quietly.

The soldiers obeyed the order, raising their Rovla rifles in unison.

Nev looked over to Miller. "Call Gilroy, Chief. Tell him to send a transmission to Horne, and then come get us."

Miller grabbed a radio from his pocket. "Hey, wake up. Send the signal."

In the cockpit, Miller's voice woke Gilroy from a nap. A signal appeared on the radar. He pushed the radio button. "Got it."

Gilroy sent the transmission to Horne. The engine lit.

"Brutton, McRae, stand guard," Nev said.

The two soldiers nodded.

The Adelpa 2 appeared and landed. Nev and the rest of the soldiers made their way toward it.

"You see anything?" McRae said.

Brutton squinted. "No."

A growl from the grass. It sounded close to them, and Brutton and McRae both took a step back.

⅄

A strong wind blasted the soldiers in the face, swirling dust all around them. Nev spat and waved his hand. He looked up into the Adelpa 2 cockpit to see Gilroy pointing to the high grass.

Nev turned to see that Brutton and McRae weren't there. He held his hand over his brow. "Lagler, O'Meara, come with me."

⅄

There was splattered blood and pieces where Brutton and McRae had been standing, as if they'd been torn apart limb from limb. The soldiers aimed their weapons readily.

"McRae! Brutton!" Nev shouted.

There wasn't a response, only the wind. A trail of steaming blood led into the high grass. The men tightened their grips on their weapons.

Seconds later, there were growls, hundreds of them, and a wave of noise. Lagler and O'Meara backed up, leaving Nev a few paces ahead.

Nev stared into the high grass. "We're going in."

"Too much blood, sir," O'Meara said.

Nev looked over at him, shocked at his soldier's hesitance.

"I think he's right, sir," Lagler said.

Nev looked back to the swirling high grass. They could board the Adelpa 2 and make a strafing run, but Nev didn't know what exactly was in that high grass. They might kill McRae and Brutton if they were still alive, or possibly the missing soldiers, those they were meant to find. He wished he had the Shoulder Devils with him.

He let the situation sink in. He had to make the best tactical decision to accomplish the mission. O'Meara was the medic. If he didn't think it was worth proceeding, Nev needed to respect that. He'd selected his men because they were exceptional soldiers. They'd have to return. "Fall back."

The men faced the high grass and quickly moved away.

Nev grabbed his radio mic. "Extraction main, extraction one."

⅄

Back at the complex, Jenkins threw down his magazine and put the mic up to his ear. "Extraction main."

Nimbus was instantly at his side and turned the speaker on so he could hear too.

⅄

"Roger, extraction main. Have a sit-rep. Found breadcrumbs. Didn't locate missing soldiers. Encountered hostiles, break…Missing two solders. How copy, over?"

No response.

"How fucking copy? Over!"

"Wilco," Jenkins voice cracked over the radio.

"Need you to focus, Jenkins."

"Yes, sir."

⅄

Nimbus leaned forward. "What kind of hostiles?"

Jenkins nodded. "Roger, say again, hostiles?"

⅄

"Will give full briefing upon return. On our way back to the complex now. Extraction one, out."

The soldiers filed inside the Adelpa 2. Nev took one more look at the high grass and then followed them.

As the aircraft ascended, the distinctive sounds of animals feeding came from the grass forest.

Onboard, no one spoke.

"Captain," Gilroy said.

"Yes?"

"Probes, dozens of them."

Nev looked out the window. Hundreds of the flying creatures were already in pursuit and destroying the probes. They flew directly into their path, sacrificing themselves to take them out.

"This is our chance," Miller said.

"Do it," Nev said.

Miller fired a wall of lead, turning the creatures into pops of bloody spray, inadvertently shooting down a few probes in the process.

"Timely," Nev said.

"Yes, Captain," Miller said.

Half the probes made it to the surface, scouring and collecting data.

⅄

Nimbus was in the complex garage. He inserted a key into the side of the mini-mobile, opening a compartment at the bottom, and loaded a case inside it.

Chapter 8

Nev closed the door to an office in the operations center and sat in front of the video feed. Colonel Horne was on the other end. He looked irritated.

"Sir," Nev said.

"Yes, Captain, what have you got?"

"I assume you're aware of the probes that made it to the surface?"

"Recording data now. Nice work, Captain."

"Thank you, sir. We encountered resident animals at a grass forest. I suspect they're related to why the soldiers went missing. Two of my squad were attacked at the site and were most likely KIA."

"Did you see them?"

"I saw their remains."

"Not them, the animals."

"No, but I heard them."

"Anything else?"

"Nothing relevant."

Horne nodded thoughtfully. Pursing his lips. "Because of your recent findings, and the success of the probes, your mission is nearly accomplished. All you need to do now is drop the minimobile at that site, so its internal beacon can display landing coordinates."

"Sir, I request permission to search the high grass with a Devil over my shoulder. I didn't find the soldiers, and because of my own…"

"I understand."

"These animals...I have the feeling they're quite formidable."

"It's not your mission, son. You've laid the groundwork. Now others will take over if necessary."

"If necessary?"

"Excuse me, Captain? Watch your tone."

Nev clenched his jaw. "No excuse, sir. I apologize."

"If those probes don't report anything pertinent, I'm going to send in a battalion."

"Request permission to lead that battalion?"

"It's a possibility. First brief your soldiers, accomplish your mission, and get back to Fort Beckett."

"Yes, sir."

"Out."

The feed went dark.

Nev briefed the men. Going home after they dropped off the mobile was good news, but it didn't change morale after losing McRae and Brutton. They were a tight squad and had worked together for years.

They always looked forward to going home, but they were soldiers. Being immersed in the shit was how they chose to live their lives. Nev knew his soldiers well, in a way that loved ones never could, and he saw in their eyes the part of every man that wanted to fight.

Almost all of their weapons, except for side arms and the ones in the armory, were loaded onto the minimobile. Nev was taking the SDs this time too. He wasn't going to make the same mistake and be unprepared again.

Nev had his orders, but he was planning on deviating from them in the way he'd learned to over his entire career in the military, which was to make decisions that would accomplish a personal objective in an invisible manner. They might have to poke around in the grass a bit before heading back to the rear, as a safety precaution, of course. He was sure his men wouldn't mind.

Chapter 9

Since no one was staying behind, Lagler gave Jenkins minimobile duty. He was happy to accept the mission—anything to get off the radio. Its engine hummed ahead of them and rolled over the terrain with ease.

The squad was dressed in full battle rattle. Nimbus wore armor too, but he didn't carry a weapon. The group moved down the slope where the Cryton boat was docked.

Nev cursed silently. The landscape was barely visible through the thick morning fog, and he wondered how difficult it would be to find the Adelpa 2 after another damn boat ride. It would be about thirty meters past the water.

They'd almost cleared the flat ground that led down the hill when suddenly a one-ton quadruped leapt over a dirt bank and landed ahead of the minimobile. The men froze in their tracks. The minimobile whined to a stop.

"Is that one of them?" Clark said.

It barely could be seen through the fog, but its height loomed over them, even from a distance. The animal let out a low grunt with each breath and stepped toward them. They could see the outline of it, its long teeth and shadowed eyes.

"It's a Ravager. From your high grass, Captain," Nimbus said, and he slowly raised his camera to chest level and took a photo.

The sound of the camera made the Ravager lower its head and growl. It reared up and pounced the dirt. The men were statues. There was a bark from somewhere out of view, and more appeared near the first.

Nev glanced at the minimobile. Where the SDs were. What he needed. The beast was watching him, and it moved closer as if it could read Nev's mind. "Fire!"

The soldiers fired their weapons. It was natural for the first shots fired to miss, so the Ravagers seemed to be more startled by the noise. Then the bullets found their mark, and the animals snarled and ran toward them.

Nev waved his hand. "Back to the complex now!"

The group turned and ran as fast as humanly possible. Jenkins lunged at Nev, butting him with his shoulder, moments before a Ravager appeared and swiped into him with both of its front paws, ripping through his armor. Blood flew in ropes. Nev stopped to help him, but Jenkins's head had been bitten off.

Nev fired his Rovla, and one of the other soldiers pulled him by the armor. He turned and scrambled for the complex. Another Ravager came by at full speed, stealing Jenkins's body.

Nev shot a glance behind him to see there were even more galloping after them. "Move! Move! Move!"

Lagler slammed against the complex. "Two eight one five nine zero."

The door opened.

The men fired in random directions as they ran into the complex. Nev flipped the main-door switch. It was closing when one of the creatures got half of itself inside. It plunged its right claws into Clark's thigh. The men grabbed his hands and arms. Nev pulled his tactical knife.

The animal pulled Clark from their grip and threw him to the others. It whipped its head back inside, snarling. Nev slammed his knife through its skull with a crunch.

The Ravager dropped to the floor, and blood poured down its face. It was a fearsome beast and similar to an Earth lion in appearance, but it didn't have any fur. Its massive teeth dripped saliva. The neck rose steeply to the top of its back, and the creature was white, with dark stripes covering it. Half inside the complex, it was five feet to the top of its shoulder blades, dead on its belly. It had small ears.

The carcass was rapidly yanked out, too quickly for the men to finish their morbid inspection. As the door closed, the men fell to the ground, sat, and kneeled, catching their breaths.

"How did they find us?" Gilroy said.

No one answered.

From outside, Clark screamed.

"What the fuck? He's still alive!" Grady said. His expression pleaded with Nev. He eyed the closed door. "He's still alive!" Grady rushed the door.

"Don't be stupid," Lagler said.

Nev quickly immobilized Grady in a chokehold. "You're going to jeopardize the rest of your squad?"

Grady breathed hard.

"Think," he said.

Grady relaxed. Nev released him and took his pistol out of its holster. He flipped the switch that closed the secondary bar door and then opened the main door. The men moved to see.

"They're ripping him apart!" Grady said.

The animals turned.

"They want us to try to save him," Nev said, controlling his anger. He fired three shots, killing Clark. The Ravagers tore into him immediately.

"You are all going to fucking die!" Grady yelled.

One trotted over and stood directly in front of the door, barking and snarling.

Grady held up his middle finger. "Fuck you!"

Nev fired. The Ravager dodged right, and the bullet punched into another's shoulder, one that was feeding on Clark's body. It howled and glared at Nev. Its lips peeled back to show its massive bloodstained teeth. A dozen of them moved toward the doorway. Nev flipped the switch, and the door closed. The complex shuddered from them ramming it.

"What are we going to do, sir?" O'Meara said.

"We need the minimobile. The rest of our weapons…Lagler?"

Lagler's eyes widened. "Jenkins had it, sir."

Nev thought in silence for a moment. "OK, Sergeant. We'll deal with it later. Nimbus," he said, getting his attention. "In here."

Nimbus followed Nev into an office.

⅄

"Tell me what you know," Nev said.

Nimbus's brow furrowed. "About?"

"When you were here."

"Nothing happened while I was here."

"What about after you left?"

"After I left, the men here said they encountered those animals. Called them Ravagers, because of the way they killed."

"Why didn't you warn us?"

"I only overheard it. I didn't know for sure."

Nev stepped toward him. "It would have been nice to know before we went out there!"

"Why the hell do you think you're here?"

"You should have mentioned it."

"Talk to Horne! It isn't up to me to relinquish top-secret information. He probably thought the attacks were uncommon."

Nev's eyes narrowed. "Why send you then? As a biologist, if there were any way to help us, telling me what you just said would have been it."

"I'm here to document the wildlife that we encounter and report all findings back to Colonel Horne."

"So this is a vacation for you?"

"How long have we been on this planet? Don't you think every outing should be detailed and recorded to help future missions?"

"What did you do before you were a biologist?"

"That's irrelevant."

"Not to me. What did you do?"

"Oh, I didn't tell you?"

"No! You didn't!"

"That's because it's none of your fucking business!"

Nev breathed hard. He was seconds away from grabbing Nimbus by the neck.

Nimbus obviously saw it coming and took a step back, putting up his hands. "I'm sorry for your losses, Captain. I am. I'm sorry for what happened. However, you have to stay focused. I'm not the reason for all this. Those animals are."

Nev caught his breath. Then he relaxed and nodded. "Do you think they came here because of the incident at the high grass? Because we entered their territory or something?"

Nimbus let his hands drop to his sides. "Most likely. They're clearly predators. Predators are territorial. They probably followed your breadcrumbs, and they're able to swim."

"That was miles away. They must be incredibly fast."

"Unfortunately."

⅄

Outside, the Ravagers could be heard grunting and barking to one another.

"Don't they ever shut up?" Grady said. He stood in front of the closed door. "Shut the fuck up!"

"Calm down, Grady," Lagler said.

"Why should I?"

"Because I said so, Private!"

"You think I give a shit about rank right now? I'm fucking older than you!"

"Calm down, Grady," Nev said as he and Nimbus rejoined the group. "Don't lose your military bearing. You need to listen to your new section chief. Got it?"

Grady stared back at him, mentally adjusting. "Got it, sir." Grady turned to Lagler and nodded.

"Listen up," Nev said. "We make our way to the mobile and get the rest of our weapons, fight our way to the Adelpa, drop the mobile at the site, and make it back to Fort Beckett. Too easy." Nev looked to the door. "I think this door can open and shut fairly quickly. I want to take a peek. Grady."

"Yes, sir?" Grady said eagerly, motivated by any hint of revenge.

"I want you to open and then close this door as fast as you can."

Grady went to the control panel, and Nev put his nose to the door. Grady flipped the switch, and the door opened.

Outside, the animals snarled and launched themselves against the building with a rocking impact, harder than the last time. Nev dodged back. Grady flipped the switch, shutting the door.

There was a long silence.

"I wish we had windows," Miller said.

"I don't," Gilroy said.

"We'll wait two hours," Nev said. "If they're not gone, we're going to have to sneak around them."

"And if that's not possible?" Nimbus said.

"Then we'll hit them with everything we have in the armory. Everyone get some sleep. That's an order." Nev went to the wall and sat down.

⅄

Colonel Horne watched a live feed sent from a probe. It was in the center of Ravager territory, feet above the ground, just out of their reach. They barked, leapt, and snarled at it.

"Gotcha."

Chapter 10

Lagler opened and shut the complex door. The sun was directly over the complex and had extinguished the morning fog.

"No sign of them. Might be waiting to ambush," Lagler said.

"I'd bet on definitely," O'Meara said. "You should use us, sir."

"Not yet." Nev put in earplugs. "Just you and me. Ready?"

"Ready, sir," Lagler said.

Nev, with a Rovla, and Lagler, with a pistol and a mine layer slung over his back, went outside. Lagler shot at the surrounding dirt banks with his pistol.

Nev watched closely. No movement. "OK."

Grady pulled the switch inside, and the door shut behind them.

Lagler holstered his pistol and slid the mine layer to his front. "It's gotta be here somewhere."

"Fire them high," Nev said, pointing. "And low, six rows."

Lagler fired the mines midway up the dirt banks and at their base, placing all twelve, creating a protective sector of explosives. Both searched the ground.

"It was about here, right?" Nev said.

"Yes, sir…Got it!" Lagler bent down and picked up the minimobile remote. He blew on it and pressed a button. The top of the minimobile slid open, revealing its inner armory.

Nev hustled to it and retrieved both SD controls, activating the Devils. They rose and hovered over each shoulder. Both adjusted to Nev's aim accordingly, ominously pointed and ready for battle.

Lagler got within ten meters, and he stopped. The minimobile whined to movement, linked to the proximity of the remote. Nev stood guard, aiming the SDs.

After Lagler had reached the complex, the garage was opened for him, and he drove the mobile inside.

A grunt came from out of view, and a mine exploded, sending up a cloud of dirt and guts.

"Captain!" Lagler shouted.

"Get that door shut!" Nev yelled.

More Ravagers leapt over the dirt bank and hit the ground running. Two exploded. Nev aimed the powerful weapons toward the racing predators and squeezed both triggers. The SDs rose a few meters higher, whined their three-second delay, and fired. The explosion of rounds was deafening.

Most of the charging animals were killed in seconds. They were no match for the amount of lead that was fired through them. Some were knocked backward and hobbled before bleeding to death. A few were pounded into the dirt and killed instantly. One saw what was happening to the others and backed up cautiously but stepped on a mine.

Blood clouded the air as Nev continued to shoot at those remaining, but he quickly dodged the beasts, making sweeps inward, never losing control of his sector of fire. The SDs rose and fell accordingly.

Four left, and they paused. Nev stopped shooting. They glared at Nev, barked to one another, and fanned out.

"Fuck me."

They charged full speed from four different directions.

Nev shot the first two to the left and then aimed at the right two, killing one easily; however, the last was able to dodge his fire and come right at him.

One of the SDs stuttered, momentarily reloading. Nev backed up, squeezing out a burst of fire from the other SD with each step. The Ravager snarled. It was huge compared to him, even from a distance.

The ammo seated, and rounds filtered into the chamber.

The Ravager leapt, jaws open, massive paws extended.

Nev fired both Devils.

Its trajectory was halted when it was hit midair and blown back. It struck the ground and slid solidly across the rocky terrain before finally coming to a stop. Dust clouded around the dead beast.

As Nev approached it, he saw blood spurting from hundreds of bullet holes. Its frame was a bit smaller than the others, as if it were young. It hadn't grown into its large paws.

Nev looked over at the complex and saw Lagler waving from the main door. He'd secured the minimobile. Nev walked backward, watching the distance for more quadrupeds.

With weapons restocked and the immediate Ravager threat diminished, Nev knew they could make it to the Adelpa 2.

Lagler came up to Nev. "They were waiting for us."

Chapter 11

Nev stepped outside the complex. From inside, the men covered him as he sent his SDs to reload. Even with such powerful weapons, Nev still had a Rovla on his back, just in case.

The sun shined brightly. Visibility was excellent. It couldn't have been better for what they needed to do.

The SDs docked themselves on the ammo boxes, and bullets filtered inside each one, snug to the point where one more round couldn't fit. Then they traveled back and aligned themselves over Nev's shoulders.

The squad moved past carcasses, along the flat ground.

"Can't wait for a little R and R," Gilroy said.

"I hear that," O'Meara said.

They got to the top of the hill, and Lagler stopped. "Captain, do you see that?"

The Adelpa 2 was barely noticeable in the distance, but it was clearly in pieces.

"Oh, fuck," Grady said.

"Shit," Miller said.

Nev put a hand above his eyes to block the sun, when he saw movement from the water below. Hundreds of Ravagers, likely the ones that had destroyed the Adelpa 2, were swimming straight for them. The rest of the men saw them too. There was only a short stretch of land separating them from the lake. The men looked to Nev.

"Can we stand them off?" Lagler said.

"Nimbus, get back to the complex and keep the door open," Nev said.

"You got it," Nimbus said and ran back toward the complex.

The Ravagers emerged from the water and galloped up the hill. As they did, they fanned out with a clear plan of attack.

"Give me some cover fire," Nev said.

As the squad aimed and fired with controlled, deliberate bursts, Nev tagged Ravagers in the SD lenses. He chose the ones to their front and to their right flank, which was closest to them. Then he held the tag button and drew target lines right through the middle of them. Nev pushed the autofire button, and the SDs rose.

The churn of fired lead chewed through Ravagers like a razor through soft flesh. There were too many for Nev to kill, but he hoped the weapons would frighten them. The animals dispersed, but instead of scurrying away with fright as most animals would, they headed right for the soldiers, intent on getting their teeth and claws into those responsible for the attack.

"Fall back!" Nev shouted.

Upon the men's movement, the Ravagers, as any predator will do with fleeing prey, snarled and galloped after them.

⅄

Nimbus ran through the complex while holding a radio. "Sir, the Adelpa two is destroyed! We have no present way of reaching the Ravagers!"

From the radio, Horne's voice boomed. *"A probe was able to pinpoint the center of their territory in the dark mountains. I'm sending a battalion to handle the Ravagers at the grass forest. Try to knock down their numbers while pleasing higher."*

"Are you sending an A-brid?"

"Yes. The grid location to where I need you to drop off the minimobile is preloaded."

"What about Nev and his men?"

"Leave at least one alive to bring with you. Kill the others."

"Yes, sir!"

Nimbus entered the garage. He got a Rovla out of the minimobile before driving it into the elevator. He pushed the button for the roof and pulled the charging handle on the Rovla as the doors closed.

⅄

An Adelpa HJC, commonly referred to as an A-brid, ascended from Fort Beckett. The hybrid jet/helicopter did a short takeoff vertically. Then its engine nozzles rotated aft, and it accelerated.

⅄

At the complex, the door wasn't open as it was supposed to be.

"Lagler, get that fucking door open!" Nev shouted.

Lagler pushed numbers on the console behind them over and over. O'Meara and Grady's sector of fire was on their left. Miller and Gilroy's sector of fire was on their right. Nev tagged Ravagers straight ahead. The Shoulder Devils rose and fell, shredding the Ravagers unluckily enough to be tagged through Nev's target lens.

"It ain't happening, sir," Lagler said.

A group of Ravagers suddenly appeared to their right and bolted for them.

"Look out!" Miller said.

Nev drew lines with both controllers. Above them, both SDs descended and aligned, turning downward, and blasted, firing hundreds of rounds in a few seconds, killing the Ravagers that had nearly crashed through the soldiers' defense. Gilroy was wide-eyed.

"Lagler!" Nev said.

"Console's been damaged."

"Fuck it! I'll tear it down. All of you move forward five meters and give me half a clock of cover fire when I say." As the soldiers obeyed the order, Nev painted target lines at their front, left, and right. "Fire!"

The soldiers fired their Rovlas. Nev hit the autofire button on one of the Devil's controls, and it ascended and joined the blockade. No weapons fired at specific targets, but Ravagers bold enough to attempt to get through were torn up. Nev aimed the other Devil at the door.

The area of the entrance to the complex was a wall of fire and lead in both directions as the squad fired their weapons at the oncoming Ravagers, and Captain Nev fired into the door. The eruption of bullets toppled it inward.

"Captain!" O'Meara shouted.

Nev spun. The SD turned as well, rising above him. Lagler was being dragged away, and Grady was shooting the Ravager responsible when another one tackled him, taking his side into its mouth, turned, shook, and flung him. Grady seemed to come apart and land in two different places. The beasts converged on both, and he and Lagler were quickly the center of a feeding frenzy.

Nev raised the other controller and aimed at the sizeable pack of Ravagers heading for them. The change of aim deleted the cover-fire lines Nev had painted through the target lens. The other SD pivoted and descended, aligning itself with the other one. Nev fired both Shoulder Devils at the quickly approaching animals, dropping them with headshots and well-aimed rounds that hit them at or near their chest and backs.

Above the complex, an Adelpa HJC approached. As the engine powered down, its propeller emerged and whined into a powerful gyration. The sight of the aircraft seemed to confuse the Ravagers, and they stopped their attack. No sense wasting ammo. Nev ceased fire.

Most Ravagers in view were still, seemingly aware of the strength of the enemy before them. However, a few paced the outskirts, intent on figuring out how to get to the humans.

⅄

The men moved through the complex, turning every so often to see if the creatures had made it inside. No one acknowledged the deaths of Lagler or Grady. Fear and anger were the only active emotions among the group.

Nev aimed the controllers at the ground, and the Devils followed close to his back like mechanical wings. "Double-time it up there. I'll wait a few minutes to ensure no one gets a Ravager up his ass before he gets in the A-brid. Go!"

The men hustled up the stairs. Two more Ravagers came through the demolished door at a full gallop, huffing and growling, picking up speed with each step. Nev walked backward, aiming his weapons as he did, and fired. The bullet flashes lit up the dark hallway.

The Ravagers were knocked across the floor. Their blood trails ended when they hit the walls. It was only then that Nev's fingers came off the triggers.

Nev was about to go upstairs when he heard something step inside the hall behind him. He turned and saw a Ravager that was larger than the others, and it was alone. Thin white stripes covered it. When Nev saw it, it stopped moving. Its brow knitted into one, and its lips curled back to reveal massive teeth and dark gums.

The Ravager lowered its head and squatted low, ready to spring. It faked right but then dodged left and charged. Nev luckily guessed its move and fired. The SDs were beyond loud; the hallway multiplied each round's report exponentially.

Bullets pounded it as it tried to move backward, but the wave of headshots dropped it. It was still alive as Nev saw that the SDs were depleted of ammo. He switched the weapons off. The SDs descended to the floor.

Nev dropped the controllers and swung the Rovla forward from around his back. He aimed it at the Ravager's face as it looked up at him with intelligent eyes. Nev felt a pang of remorse before pulling the trigger.

O'Meara opened the door to the roof to see Nimbus waiting by the Adelpa HJC. He held up his hand, and O'Meara, Miller, and Gilroy did the same.

"Where's Captain Nev?" Nimbus shouted.

O'Meara cupped his hands on the sides of his mouth. "He's on his way up!"

Nimbus aimed his Rovla and shot O'Meara in the head. Miller and Gilroy raised their weapons, but they weren't fast enough, and Nimbus took them down with short, well-aimed bursts of fire.

As Nev ran for the roof, he heard shooting above him. Had the Ravagers even made it up there?

Nev opened the door to the resounding whine of the A-brid's rotating blades. Miller, Gilroy, and O'Meara lay in a large pool of their own blood.

Nev took a knee next to Miller, who was barely alive. As he gazed up at him, his eyes widened.

Nev glanced over his shoulder and saw Nimbus appear from behind the door. He came down hard with the butt of a Rovla, knocking Nev out.

Miller raised a hand. "No!"

Nimbus fired a single shot into Miller's head at point-blank range.

Chapter 12

Three Adelpa 1 transport ships landed near the high grass. The platforms lowered, and moments later, soldiers marched out.

Lieutenant Colonel Dale Pritchard chewed on a cigar while he watched his troops finish exiting the aircrafts and mobilize. He examined the landing zone. The high grass was everywhere. "Captain Nev and his men are here somewhere! We know our mission! Break down to assigned squads and move in! Maintain five-meter distance!"

The soldiers separated into squads and trudged into the grass forest. Moments later, there was yelling and gunfire. It sounded as if they were being attacked.

The soldiers who had yet to enter the high grass froze in their tracks. The ground vibrated. It was obvious that animals were heading toward them.

Ravagers launched out of the grass. Pritchard's battalion quickly formed a rank and fired. The two species clashed with the beasts towering unfairly over the humans. They tossed soldiers behind them, allowing those that weren't part of the front onslaught to get a taste of man.

A few soldiers were thrown and then tackled midair as if the Ravagers were making a sport of it. Many of the men tried to run back into the ships, but most didn't make it. Ravagers galloped after those who did, right into an Adelpa 1.

Pritchard saw it. He shot a Ravager in the face, dropping it. "Line of fire! Line of fire!"

A group of soldiers formed a defense that blocked the path into the aircraft. If they wanted to get home, Ravagers would unquestionably be considered expendable cargo. The soldiers fired.

The animals took shots to the face and fell, but it didn't deter those that were behind them. They advanced without any fear for their own lives. A few scrambled past the dead, practically using the carcasses like shields, and they took swipes at the soldiers who fired. The rear group of the creatures fanned out and advanced slowly.

Communication was impossible. The fighting was happening too quickly, and there was too much radio chatter back and forth on the same net.

Two Ravagers suddenly leveled Pritchard. They each grabbed a limb and pulled. The Lieutenant Colonel screamed. Soldiers took a step toward their superior to help, but he'd already been ripped apart.

⅄

A soldier peeked inside the aircraft and saw a Ravager mauling one of his comrades. As he did, he wasn't aware of a Ravager that stalked him from behind like a cat.

The soldier stepped into view. "Hey!"

The creature stopped feeding and looked up at him.

"Yeah, you."

It lowered its head, bared its teeth, and snarled. The soldier fired his rifle, hitting it in the chest, killing it. He turned to find a Ravager in front of him. It pounced and pushed him onto his back.

"No!"

It used its front paws to hold the soldier down. Then it plunged its teeth into his stomach and tore out pounds of flesh.

⅄

The soldiers fought their best, but it was useless. There were only a few of them left. The area was mostly moving Ravagers. The soldiers had formed a circle and aimed carefully, choosing their shots.

The Ravagers continued to move, raising and lowering their heads and accelerating when shot at. Then they closed in swiftly, like an unexpected punch, seizing soldiers' necks in their mouths.

Chapter 13

Nev woke to the vociferous rumble of the A-brid and a dull ache on the side of his head. Nimbus had hit him quite hard, but it didn't feel as if anything was broken. Shackles linked under his seat cuffed his hands in front of him. Nimbus sat behind the minimobile, staring at him. "Where are we headed?"

Nimbus was expressionless, though he did look away, which probably meant he had plans for him. Nev looked over to see they were headed toward the dark mountains. Nimbus could have killed him, but he didn't. He needed him.

"What's on the mobile?"

No response.

"You're working for Horne, so I bet he's in on it."

Nimbus turned and gazed coldly.

"I knew you were too fucking stupid to do anything on your own."

Nimbus smiled.

"What's on the mobile?"

He was getting angry.

"Come on! What's it matter?"

"Mero gas. Know it?"

Nev had never seen Mero gas, but he'd heard of it. It was an airborne biological weapon that exterminated specific races, and it was named after the lunatic who created it. Apparently, it could be used against different species too. "Why?"

"The territory."

"For who?"

"The elite."

The wealthy. So, their mission was a smokescreen. Whatever Horne reported to higher was only partially true or a lie altogether. Nev and his men were there to handle Horne and Nimbus and whoever else's personal business, paving the way for their financial gain with blood. "How many missions before this one?"

"Four."

"Military?"

"No. The first were civilian, exploration."

"How did they fare?"

"They didn't have the firepower you and your men did. It was bloody. After them, we sent soldiers."

"To their deaths." Nev yanked on his shackles. "Are you aware of what the repercussions of this will be? What it can do to an ecosystem?"

"I seem to remember you killing a few."

"I'll kill to save my own neck or protect the lives of my men, but I'd never wipe out an entire species."

They rode in silence for a while.

"You obviously can't shoot me, or you would have done it already. Though I bet you thought about it for a while, didn't you? It wouldn't make sense to whoever found my body. Even you can't be that stupid."

Nev could see waves of anger flowing over him. Nimbus didn't like being called stupid. Who would?

"Smothering me might work. You were probably already thinking something along those lines, or Horne suggested it to you...Might as well do it now. What's your plan once we get there? Politely ask the Ravagers to mind their own business while I don't fight back as you kill me?" he said and laughed.

The men stared at each other. If Nimbus had planned on killing Nev all along, it would have been too easy to drug him while he was unconscious. The fact that he was still alive meant that he and Horne had come up with a plan recently, and it gave him a fighting chance.

"You're gonna have to do it, now or later. You man enough?"

Nimbus stood. "Let's find out."

That was unexpected. Nev thought he'd have to work on Nimbus longer to piss him off. He bet Nimbus had the keys to his shackles on him. He'd have to figure out a way to get to them once he was close.

Lucky for him, Nimbus approached him from the far side, the way he hoped. He could see Nimbus was getting a punch ready. He'd probably try to knock him out and then kill him whichever way he'd already decided.

Nev ducked the punch and wrapped his legs around him, twisting enough to topple him over. Nimbus came down hard and hit the back of his head. He was out.

Nev had enough slack to bend down and fish around in his left pocket, but he couldn't find any keys. They had to be on him somewhere. Around his neck maybe? If they were, it was impossible to reach. Nev thought for a moment. He had to be fast. Nimbus wouldn't be unconscious for long, and the pilot hadn't noticed what had happened.

Nev hoped what he needed was on the side closest to him. He reached out with his heel and nudged the drawer at the bottom of the minimobile. It opened and slid out. Nimbus must not have known about the tools that came equipped. If he did, he wouldn't have sat Nev on the same side or so close.

Nev's view was minimal from where he was sitting, but then he caught sight of a laser torch. He scooted out as far as he could on his butt and put his heels together. He dropped them in the drawer and dug around until he got a secure grip. Then he squeezed them together, raising them up.

Nimbus stirred. Nev held the tool between his heels and brought it out. He dropped it beneath him and reached down. He turned it on, and its white fire burned hot. He held the heat to his shackle, and seconds later, he was able to free his right hand. He did the same thing to the other side, and he was free. He got up and pulled the pistol that was in Nimbus's holster and put it to his head.

Nimbus expertly knocked the weapon out of his grasp, to Nev's surprise. He'd come to within the last few seconds. Nev saw his eyes adjust. Nimbus followed the swipe with a lightning-quick elbow to Nev's face. Nev dropped to a knee, holding his nose. He wouldn't have allowed that to happen if he'd known Nimbus was conscious. Nimbus took off his jacket.

"You weren't always a civilian," Nev said, getting to his feet.

The pilot turned briefly.

"Just keep flying!" Nimbus said.

Both spied the pistol just out of reach. Nev lunged, but Nimbus grabbed him and threw him against the wall. Nev chopped his right arm, grabbed his wrist, and twisted him to the floor. Nimbus pulled from Nev's grip, rocked, and flipped onto his feet. He punched Nev's blood-spattered face. Nev kicked him in the chest, causing the air to be expelled from his lungs. Nev lunged for the gun again and missed. Nimbus leapt on top of him.

The Adelpa HJC looked as small as a speck of pepper as it flew toward the massive, dark mountains.

It thundered along the terrain, moving over a murky, tree-filled swamp. Below was a fat, gluttonous, brown beast with an open mouth that was tilted toward the sky. It grumbled and rolled into the water with a giant splash.

Nev reached back and locked his arm over Nimbus's arm and rolled him, giving Nev the opportunity to escape his clutches.

Nev stood and quickly shot out a kick that scuffed Nimbus across the face, briefly stunning him. Nimbus stood and smiled, a sure sign he'd been hurt. The two men interlocked and grappled, trying to overpower the other with expertly delivered short blows to each other's neck, face, and body.

Both were bloody, but Nimbus's jaw jutted awkwardly, probably broken from the kick. They both got a hand on the pistol at the same time, and it shot twice, and the third round crashed through the back of the pilot's helmet. He was dead, but he still had hold of the controls, and the Adelpa HJC dipped.

The pistol fell to the floor between them. Nimbus reached for it, but Nev punched him hard, and Nimbus stumbled a step back, involuntarily giving Nev the chance to punch with his right and left, and he kicked upward with his right foot, directly into Nimbus's chest, launching him near the open door. Nev reached down and grabbed the pistol.

Nimbus stood. "Don't suppose you'd finish my mission for me?"

Nev aimed. "Missions are for soldiers," he said, and he fired six rounds as fast as he could pull the trigger.

Nimbus fell backward out of the plunging aircraft.

Below, dark shapes scrambled away seconds before Nimbus hit the water.

When he broke the surface, he could barely move. His back felt odd, like it was bent. Behind him, a large hump rose. Then a reptilian face appeared in front of it. The creature opened its wide, needle-teeth-filled mouth, and as quick as a snapping rattlesnake, it took Nimbus in its jaws and dove. Its long, whiplike tail thrashed powerfully, accelerating the creature downward to the swamp's cold, murky depths.

As the A-brid plummeted, Nev tried to stay on his feet, but he fell. He got up again and looked out the door. The ground and swamp were approaching quickly, but he knew if he jumped too high, he could be paralyzed. Water was like concrete from a certain height.

He waited a few more seconds and then leapt out.

The impact rendered him momentarily unconscious, and he began to sink. Recognizing he was underwater Nev jolted awake and sprang upward. A dark shape swum below him.

When he broke the surface, he took deep breaths and coughed. He spied the nearby shore and swam for it. He heard an explosion behind him and turned to see the A-brid had smashed into a mountainside and was now a smoky fireball.

A hump broke the surface in his eye line. Upon sight of it, he sped up his crawl stroke and stood up when the water was shallow enough. He hustled onto shore. When he turned, he saw the creature cease its hunt and dive. Its tail whipped.

Nev collapsed from exhaustion, blood oozing down his face. The swamp was putrid and ugly. A slimy substance coated everything in sight.

A stiff wind blew and skittered mini waves, spraying Nev with a light mist. He shivered uncontrollably and looked up. A dark mountain rose steeply before him, so large it looked as if it might weigh the planet down. He couldn't see the top.

Chapter 14

A walking stick aided Nev in hiking to higher ground. He'd covered the inside of his clothes with dry moss he'd initially intended to help dry him faster, but it was making him rather warm with all the strenuous movement. So warm, in fact, that he considered taking it out. He stopped a moment to rest and was surprised to see steam pouring out of his clothing.

Nev had been a soldier for half of his life and had grown accustomed to mentally chewing on thoughts and ideas that kept him occupied. The ones he was thinking troubled him. He didn't know if the laws of nature from Earth applied all throughout the universe or if it were natural for a superior species to wipe out an inferior one, which was itself a subjective opinion.

Nev knew it was expected for humans to explore, but exploration often meant annihilation. In this instance, the draw was the planet's beauty and its similarities to Earth, a rather petty motivation.

Tuhrelevim felt like Earth; even Nev sensed it, and he'd never been there. His grandfather had, though. He'd wanted to see Earth before he died. Nev's own feeling of familiarity, aside from history and pictures, was something embedded in his DNA.

Tuhrelevim wasn't Earth. It was an entirely new world, and if their mere presence caused conflict, how much of a right did they have to be there in the grand scheme of things?

Nev exhaled. He understood how things were, but he hated the guilt that surfaced from being human, no matter how much was rationalized or explained to him.

⅄

Nev had reached the top of a peak that he'd thought was rather high, only to see another that was a bit higher before him. He grunted to himself and headed toward it, continuing to travel the opposite way of the dark mountains. He hoped he'd be able to use triangulation at some point, enough to recognize where he was the closer he got to the complex, and get his ass back to Fort Beckett.

The ride on the A-brid had taken him at least thirty klicks away from the complex—a five-hour hump, minimum, and that too, if he didn't run into any Ravagers or anything else. He kept thinking of them, too, especially the last one he'd killed in the complex before he went to the roof.

It seemed different from the others. Nev was smart enough to recognize hierarchy. That one seemed like it was in charge, or at least it was one of the leaders. He remembered seeing others like it at the outskirts of their groupings, surveying the area. The Ravagers probably had a ranking system that was like the military. Whether he'd killed the main Ravager leader—something he doubted the more he thought about—he didn't know.

Humans shouldn't insert themselves so violently. They should mosey on in respectfully. His thought made him laugh out loud, and his wife would get a kick out of what he thought. He missed her. He needed to get back to her.

He could just disappear. He'd been in the military since he was eighteen and hadn't fallen into the financial traps that beset most soldiers at that age. He'd always been smart with his money, and he had plenty of it. Besides that, no one knew he was alive. Except he couldn't just let what happened go. There was no way the mission was approved by higher authority. This was the Colonel acting on his own, and it wouldn't fly on Earth, but they were a long way from Earth.

Out here, the idea of military justice was a joke. The military was spread too thin over too many planets, and most soldiers were on the brink of becoming mercenaries. There wasn't much to stop them. Nev was probably seeing the last remnants of an organized military. Having those responsible rot in prison wouldn't make a difference.

Horne couldn't be allowed to go unpunished. He would continue to put soldiers' lives at risk. He had too much power and had too many friends. He'd been a soldier for decades. An officer with such a high rank could blame those below him, particularly Nev. Something had to be done about it. Nev could do something. He should just kill him. If they could do what they wanted, why couldn't he?

Nev didn't want to start a war, though. It could put his wife in danger. It would have to be done quietly. Nev had done *quietly* before, and he could do it again. The Colonel hadn't been outside the wire in a long time. Complacency was a reliable and effective advantage.

Part 2

Operation Tuhrelevim

Chapter 15

The Tactical Operations Center at Fort Beckett was bustling as mission preparations were made. There were soldiers who were actually busy and soldiers who did their best to look it under the watchful eye of Sergeant Major Kayner—otherwise they'd get their asses chewed.

Colonel Horne had invested a lot of time to make Tuhrelevim happen. The complexes that the civilian explorers had demanded were all abandoned due to the unforeseen encounters with the Ravagers. Unfortunately, the money required to build them was where the bulk of the initial expenditures of the mission had gone. That money would have been useful now, but it was spent, and nothing could take that back now. Tuhrelevim's vegetation was no doubt taking back the buildings themselves. Captain Nev and his men were the last Horne had allowed to stage at them.

The unforeseen. That summed up space travel in a nutshell. Unlimited issues with equipment, vehicles, weapons, and even people. There were all kinds of names for what happened to humans when they went from planet to planet, usually with "disorder" added to the end of it so drug companies could create a pill that magically solved that particular affliction. When a "disorder" happened to soldiers, they were told to drive on, drink water, suck it up. They were told the reason they felt the way they did was because of the time they spent away from loved ones.

Depression was a commonly used umbrella term, and convenient, because what was actually happening to them had never been properly diagnosed.

Horne knew what it was, why most people felt the way they did. There was no name for it yet, but it was simply this: humans belonged on Earth, and anywhere else was unnatural.

Horne knew this, made it his life's mission, tried to get others to see it, too, and because Earth was no longer an option, Tuhrelevim was second best. Familiarity was essential to human survival. Not a bare rock in the dark asshole of space as most planets were, Planet Tuhrelevim was essential to human survival now, a stepping-stone, at least until there were further generations of the human species who had a new definition of "familiar."

Until then, humans would be sick without Earth—where the species had most likely originated—an unavoidable affliction all people would have to deal with until their death. Horne had done his best to try to get others to see that. Sergeant Major Kayner and Major Makada seemed to understand. They weren't privy to what he'd done illegally. They didn't need to be. They were both moral, upstanding men who lived and breathed the military, and every decision had weight. If they knew that all directions from off-planet were either manipulated or fabricated by Horne, they might try to halt what needed to be done. Only Nimbus had known what was going on entirely, something required due to his mission, but that was only up to the point where he'd left with Captain Nev.

Many more people were involved in the mission now; it had a life of its own, which created more opportunities for Horne to disguise his actions. He had a lot to answer for and would address everything he had to once the Adelpa 4s—the population ships—arrived. He was far enough ahead, sanctioning and hiring and burying evidence under the classification of top secret, that he'd only get himself into trouble if the mission failed or if the ones who were killed had somehow figured everything out before that and then came back to life and exposed him. Since that wasn't likely—Ravagers didn't leave survivors—it was worth the risk. Anyway, everything he was doing was necessary.

Net traffic from higher and what Horne reported for delegation were very different. He knew in the end, all of the deception would be worth it. After Operation Tuhrelevim was a success, he doubted anybody would be asking questions. He'd make sure of it, eliminating trails to those questions to the best of his ability. The only question anybody would ask then would be where to place his monument.

There were family members on base who were demanding answers, but until they knew exactly what had transpired, the mission was classified. Captain Nev's wife had become quite the nuisance. The population was incoming, investigations needed to be *dealt* with, and the Ravager threat was still present. So they still had a few weeks before "classified," "top secret," and "under investigation" would no longer put off family inquiries.

Meanwhile, Horne, Kayner, and Makada were in charge of making Tuhrelevim safe. Makada's and Kayner's involvement happened after the events surrounding Pritchard's battalion. This was something Horne had been pushing for all along; he just didn't know it would be the result of something so terrible. As far as anyone knew, all of Pritchard's soldiers were dead. There were no more probes to send, which meant that without a soldier's direct physical line of sight, they were blind. Horne and Pritchard had been friends for a long time. His feelings of loss had been real.

Mission first, though. Always the mission first.

The small amount of coffee left in Horne's cup had gone cold as he'd been mulling over his responsibilities and all that needed to be done. He drank it anyway. Then he stood and stared out his office window at the tall cliffs that surrounded Fort Beckett. He'd chosen the natural fortress wisely—as wisely as choosing Makada and Kayner to run his base for him. Their presence—especially Makada's—increased the soldiers' productivity. Both were very intimidating with long, impressive careers. They were both lifers, like Horne. Adding them to the equation, their direct involvement, made his command that much stronger.

Horne also respected them. They were straight shooters, and they'd been serving together off and on over the years, following one another's careers. Horne had wanted them for Tuhrelevim since the beginning, but he'd had to wait for them to be available. Fortunately, after a few influential phone calls, Kayner and Makada had arrived together. After the initial briefing where

Horne underlined the bullet points about how important he felt the mission would be for humanity, they were on board from then on.

The small number of soldiers meant that missions usually reserved for those of higher rank were being delegated downward, even for Horne, which was especially frustrating. His mission was usually reserved for a general, not a fucking colonel. After Tuhrelevim was a success, he had no doubt he'd be promoted.

Even with the bare-bones chain of command, Horne was confident in the establishing personnel, including the mission failures, as well as the rest of the officers, NCOs, and soldiers who would arrive on the subsequent Adelpa 4 chalks. There were four since he'd last checked. The first pop-ship was set to arrive shortly. Because of that Tuhrelevim needed to be secured. The casualty rate—not counting the civilian exploration groups—has been too high, especially after what happened to Pritchard's battalion. The losses were unacceptable, and Horne would do his best to prevent them in the future.

The deaths didn't fall on his shoulders—although technically they did, of course—but he wouldn't be held responsible for them. All personnel signed a copious number of documents to get here. Risk was clearly marked on every page. They knew what was at stake to be here. Deaths are often *necessary* sacrifices, and deep down all soldiers knew that the sacrifice might be theirs—impossible to avoid in a war theater. Encountering dangerous life on an unexplored planet was nothing new and practically expected.

Horne's own push to ignite key aspects of Operation Tuhrelevim was unrelated to those losses, and from his perspective irrelevant. He wasn't the first human to set foot on Tuhrelevim. Who was more at fault: the one who sets the fire, or the ones unwilling to put it out?

The TOC was located next to Horne's office. Even though he had a radio at his desk, he'd requested thin walls. He still liked to hear what was going on, to feel it. At present, a young soldier was getting his ass chewed by Makada. Horne quietly opened the door to his office, peeking out into the TOC, just to get a dose of who he commanded, thankful he was no longer a young soldier himself.

Makada was standing next to the radio-transmitter operator, the RTO. "*Zero!* Not oh! Are you a soldier or a civilian?"

"Civilians don't have uniforms, sir."

Horne saw Makada's satisfaction. The soldier had sprung his trap, and soon everyone could hear the young man's exasperated breaths as he did push-ups while Makada stood over him. There'd been a lot more yelling since Makada and Kayner had taken over. It was a way those in charge asserted themselves within the chain of command so soldiers below them knew where to fall in. Even if you weren't the one getting chewed out, everyone had ears, thus dominance was established. Verbally abusing underlings was common practice in the military. It had probably always been that way, and it probably always would be.

"One, sir! Two, sir! Three—"

"Shut up!" Makada said. "Just push so you can listen."

"Yes, sir," he said and then silently continued the push-ups.

"You need to voice proper numerical net description, but also do not say 'repeat'! This is an artillery battalion. 'Repeat' is what you say for additional launches, and we don't need additional launches. To reiterate you say, 'I say again.' Understand?"

"Yes, sir!"

"I hear you say repeat on the *fucking* radio again, and I'll make sure you never get promoted, Private."

"Yes, sir," he said, his arms trembling as he continued to push.

The radio squawked.

"Permission to recover, sir?"

"Recover. Be grateful for that radio. It just saved your ass. I was just getting warmed up."

"Yes, sir." The RTO stood, red-faced, and pushed the mic. "This is Fire Direction Main, over."

"Fire Direction Main, this is Fire Direction Alpha, radio check, over."

The RTO breathed heavily, composed himself: "Loud and clear, out."

Makada turned and looked over the TOC, searching for anyone else he could smoke. Soldiers of lesser rank went about their duties nervously, careful not to make eye contact or catch his attention in any way.

Makada did catch Kayner's amusement, though. Makada gave him a half smile. "Are we doing anything, Sergeant Major?"

"Eventually," Kayner said. "I'm sure of it."

"I'd rather it be sooner than that. *We* should be planning something."

"You said that yesterday, sir."

"I hate waiting."

"Want me to call next door, rile 'em up, get some extra training going?"

"What kind of training?"

"You tell me, sir."

Makada looked down and then up. "Combat readiness."

Kayner grabbed a phone—the old land line kind from Earth, with a cord—and waited for the RTO to pick up on the other end.

"Put somebody on who knows something!...You don't know who knows something? What do you think Captain Sharvech will say when I tell him you don't think he knows anything? Don't be sorry, Specialist, just tell him I'm on my way, and you get ready to get smoked."

Kayner hung up.

"Attention!" the RTO said, and stood.

The entire TOC went to the position of attention, frozen in place. The radios continued to squawk with various, ongoing missions.

"Carry on," Horne said, standing just beyond his doorway.

All TOC personnel resumed their missions.

Horne eyed Makada and Kayner. "Gentlemen."

⅄

Horne pushed a button on his desk, and the windows went from clear to foggy, for privacy when he needed it. "First things first. The results of Dr. Nimbus's findings and also the briefing."

He left it at that, waiting for them to respond. From their chairs in front of his desk, they looked to each other.

Makada spoke for them both. "The documents for your eyes only, sir. We read them."

Of course the details about the Mero gas had been omitted.

"Good. And?"

"We've got a serious fucking problem, sir."

"I'll say."

"With those pop-ships incoming, unfortunately us people take precedence. We've gotten to the point where extermination is our only option."

"Agreed," Horne said. "That's why you're here."

"Mission first, sir," Makada said. "I believe in that, but I'm not here to be cannon fodder."

Horne understood Makada was referring to the classified details of Pritchard's failed mission.

"Nor am I," Kayner said.

"We're here to make a difference," Makada said.

Horne rolled his eyes. "Your integrity isn't in question and won't be, but did you read the *fucking* briefing? The results of Lieutenant Colonel Pritchard's mission changes things. Obviously. Operation Tuhrelevim will continue with *artillery strikes*, but then *follow* with a battalion. To kill stragglers. Then more artillery if necessary, but I assure you, it won't be."

"And if you're wrong, sir?" Kayner said.

"About what?"

"Artillery, battalion, artillery."

"Then we'll send another battalion after that."

"Who's leading the next wave, sir?" Makada said.

"After the artillery is launched, directly supervised by yourselves, Lieutenant Colonel Mathis will lead the next battalion." Before Makada could open his mouth to ask a question, Horne added, "Your further involvement will be determined then."

Makada nodded.

"We owe it to the soldiers who were lost," Kayner said, "to the soldiers who are on their way now, and their families that are incoming, to exterminate those beasts. Sir."

"I agree," Horne said. He looked over at Makada who was leaning forward in his chair, eager for his own involvement. "How are we on metal?"

Kayner answered for him. "Ready to rock, sir."

The decimation of Pritchard's battalion spurred Horne to ready his heavy weaponry: Adelpa launchers with coordinated, linked multiple-launch capability, A-brids, M331a2 weapon systems, commonly referred to as Shoulder Devils, and other sophisticated and catastrophic weapons of war that he deemed necessary for Operation Tuhrelevim to succeed.

"Now if you'll excuse me gentlemen, I need to brief Mathis."

They stood. *"Yes, sir."*

Chapter 16

Nev kept on the move. The complex was about 1,500 klicks from Fort Beckett, and the A-brid had taken them well past that. He was guessing he was at least 1,700 klicks away, and that was a long way on foot. He wasn't sure how long he'd been gone. Weeks. Less than a month. No telling how long it would take to get back, though.

What he'd initially thought was a star turned out to be the population ship. The pill-shaped Adelpa 4 aircraft was still a good distance out, but he could see it moving, close enough to put everyone on board in danger. Anyone even remotely near this planet was.

He'd triangulated his position on the basis of the maps he'd studied. They were constantly updated digitally, and the print versions were available whenever they were essential, so Nev had seen many of them. He'd learned to memorize details early in his career. As a private, he'd once forgotten vital mission information and was punished for it. Ever since then, he made sure he memorized all essential information—including what others knew—for all current missions. He could brain-dump everything he'd had to retain once the mission was over.

Of course, there was no way to retain every aspect of a mission or to know everything, either. That could cause pertinent information to be forgotten, so he would only learn what was absolutely necessary. Some details always stayed in his mind, though, even when the mission was over. If they lingered, then he figured there was some part him that thought it could still be useful.

When Nev closed his eyes, he could see a thousand miles north of Fort Beckett, up to where the complex was and a little more, as if he were looking at a map directly. It turned out that "little more" was where he was.

The depressions he was looking at didn't look natural. Just like the ones they'd run across during the mission. He recalled an unusually large number of impact sites forming a straight line next to three large mountains. He was guessing, but unless there were other areas in the territory surrounding Fort Beckett with just as many depressions next to three mountains, he was heading in the correct direction. Although considering how badly Horne wanted Tuhrelevim, it was possible there were more.

Though confident in his course, he wasn't sure how far he'd gone or how much farther Fort Beckett was. He knew with the right supplies and equipment, he could make it eventually, but what was going to give him trouble was the lack of water—he didn't want to venture too close to anything local, not after what he'd seen take Nimbus—and he'd recently run out of purifying pills. He was now only going on what he had in him.

The terrain was tough too. Nev had done PT to stay in shape his entire military career and gone on long road marches in training and on missions, but nothing he'd ever done compared to this. He hadn't slept much either. That was sapping his strength, too, and due to the lack of everything, he was the perfect target for wildlife.

Just over a hill he saw something that made everything that he'd been trying to ignore come rushing back to him as if he were injected by all of it at once: hunger, thirst, sore muscles, the painful blisters on his feet, fatigue, anger, but most important, getting back to Kate. It allowed him to acknowledge all of the things hindering him and then mentally get a hold of them again. It was a hover skiff.

It occurred to Nev that something had caused the drivers to abandon the skiff. He scanned the distance in all directions but didn't see a threat. In fact, he saw no movement at all. His gut told him it was because he must still be in Ravager territory—a seemingly safe place, but quite the contrary. Whatever animal dwelled here, it had fought and killed to dominate it. If any of them discovered Nev, he was a dead man. He didn't have any weapons other than his wits, and they'd probably enjoy eating those, too.

The skiff must have been left over from one of the exploration operations Nimbus had mentioned. Nev briefly wondered what happened to them but realized it probably wasn't a very interesting mystery. They were probably eaten.

The battery looked intact. He jostled the skiff slightly, just to see if anything came loose that he couldn't see, and then shook it. It felt tight. After giving it a thorough preventative maintenance check, he found it without damage. Whoever had driven it out here had been pulled off it long ago, judging by the dried blood that covered the numerical nomenclature after *ADELPA*. Under that read *EBA*, the initials of the vehicle's designer.

Civilian design now dominated vehicular production and military aircraft, particularly that of the man responsible for the various Adelpa options: Enginsan Borovich Adelpa. Nev had heard he was so rich he even owned his own planet. It was no wonder his creations were all over Tuhrelevim. Nev wondered if Horne knew him personally. Horne surely knew *of* him. The presence of Enginsan Adelpa's creations proved that, and he no doubt was one of Tuhrelevim's investors.

Nev had never driven a skiff before, but he'd ridden on one and had watched the driver carefully. In the military it was well known that even if it wasn't your job, the responsibility might fall in your lap one day. The skiff didn't look complicated—seemed simple enough to operate. No key was necessary. Just throttle, balance, and try not to get thrown off.

It started up quickly. The solar engines wouldn't lose their power for decades. Nev was thankful for that, listening to the engine thrum and all that the thrum meant to him.

He headed toward Fort Beckett but in a roundabout way. He didn't want to risk damaging the skiff or getting it stuck. Because of his lack of survival necessities, his life depended on it. So he followed the path with the most even terrain, although it meant not traveling as the crow flies.

When the skiff hit a bump, it adjusted accordingly, hovering up—they were designed to withstand minimal impacts—and then lowering, readjusting to the appropriate height. They were rather fast. The speedometer claimed to reach speeds over one hundred miles per hour.

⅄

Nev had covered substantial distance when he came upon an open field, a tall, jagged mountain in the distance, its peak still tipped with snow. If the hover skiff had brakes instead of a slowdown throttle, he would have stomped on them after what he saw—what he'd been hoping he wouldn't see.

Hover skiffs were meant for wide-open travel, like driving a boat, so it was smart to know when and where you were going to stop. After the skiff slowed down, Nev jumped off. The skiffs were designed with a breakdown in mind, a just-in-case-the-shit-hit-the-fan factor built into them in case they needed to be worked on, envisioned with long-distance travels in mind. Enginsan Adelpa knew what he was doing. Nev took out the binoculars located in the skiff's tool compartment.

His view was constant movement. It looked like Ravagers were fighting each other. He moved the binoculars left and right and realized that wasn't what was happening. There *were* Ravagers but not as many as whatever else it was that had surrounded them, not nearly. It was a different kind of predator—something new. They were smaller than Ravagers but looked similar, except for tails that flipped endlessly, most likely an extension of their aggressive behavior.

It was difficult for Nev to comprehend what he was witnessing, and it took a few seconds for it to sink in: Ravagers being mauled and killed by this other predator. These Maulers had numbers on their side. There must have been hundreds of them and maybe only a dozen Ravagers, and the Maulers had the Ravagers surrounded.

Nev zoomed in to the shock of how the Maulers were killing the Ravagers. They bit into their throats and yanked downward, ripping them open until blood sprayed, and then the Ravagers fell. It didn't even look like they were fighting back, as if they'd given up. The Ravagers were certainly intelligent enough to understand the concept of defeat, but their acceptance of it was baffling. That wasn't like them at all.

Nev wondered if he was watching a territorial dispute. Maybe the Maulers sensed the Ravager's hold over their territory weakening after all the fighting with the humans. Maybe these Maulers won the dispute. Perhaps those Ravagers were sickly, so much so that they couldn't fight back. But all of them? That didn't seem possible, especially considering how viciously they had attacked Nev and his men.

Nev got back on the skiff and twisted the throttle as far as it would go, meaning to put as much distance between him and them as possible.

An hour later, Nev stopped to scan behind him. There was still movement, far off but coming. He doubted the Maulers were following him; there was a large herbivore in their path. He'd nearly run into it himself, mistaking it for a small hill, and then had to quickly dodge the rest of its herd. The animals were slow moving and looked like an Earth elephant without the trunk, tail, or ears and double in size.

The Maulers secluded one of the smaller animals from the group, probably an infant, and then attacked it from the front, sides, and rear—all at the same time. They were just getting it down when another Mauler leapt and landed on top of it, forcing it to the ground. Other Maulers rushed in and bit into it, driving their mouths deep into the big animal.

Several Maulers kept the herbivore's herd away, running at them and probably snarling. Nev could see their open jaws.

They were *eating* this animal, but Nev had only seen them *kill* the Ravagers. Of course, he hadn't stuck around to see what happened after the Ravagers were dead. Perhaps the Maulers ate them, too, but he doubted it. He got the feeling the Maulers were intelligent enough, as the Ravagers were, to make the distinction between hunting and killing.

Ravagers were bigger and probably stronger, but the Maulers seemed to have an advantage over the Ravagers that had helped them dominate the territory: they attacked as a group, where Ravagers separated. Though difficult to say which method was more effective, the Ravagers hadn't coordinated their attacks like that. Not even close.

Nev continued to hypothesize as he drove as fast as the skiff was capable, estimating he'd be back to Fort Beckett by tomorrow morning. Maybe the Maulers sensed a shift in Ravager numbers, and that was when they moved into their territory. Maybe the feud had gone on long before humans had even arrived on Tuhrelevim—probably—and Nev was witnessing this new predator come out on top. When the Maulers made their push, they must have done it fast. No doubt the Ravagers had dominated the territory for a long time, but the Maulers figured out a way to outmatch them somehow.

Nev was already tired of thinking about them and decided to go over what he needed to do once he got back to Fort Beckett, thoughts that had been his fuel since the A-brid crash—his prime motivation. Getting himself and his wife off-planet was his main priority, but if he could get to Horne before that...

He wouldn't want to lead any predators to the base, though. He saw a small animal and stopped to approach it on foot. It was furry and hadn't shied away from him before he bludgeoned it to death—probably curious about him, having never seen a human before. Nev hated to do it. It made him feel awful, just like everything he'd had to kill, including the Ravagers, but to get back to Kate he was willing to do anything.

Most likely, the animal was in the Mauler's diet considering how many there were in the territory. He cut off a few pieces of his uniform, placed them under its furry corpse, and then sped off in the opposite direction. He didn't think the Maulers were following him, but if they were, hopefully the ruse would throw them off his scent.

Nev heard aircraft. Aircraft meant rescue. But remembering his botched mission, the sound filled him with dread instead. They might be coming to kill him—to finish him off. But then no one knew he was still alive. Not even his wife.

He scanned the sky, trying to spot the aircraft, maybe an A-brid, only to see rockets instead. The guided homing bombs tore across the sky, their exhaust trails creating a spiral cloud in their wake, disrupting a flock of the flying creatures with upturned snouts he'd seen destroy probes.

The rockets hit somewhere in the dark mountains, the dull *thu-wump, thu-wump* of their impacts could be felt through the ground, even from Nev's distance, surely annihilating whatever lived there.

Because of the magnetic link between the multiple-launch capability of the Adelpa launchers, the stacked propulsion of all the rockets firing together meant that the distance capability of the rockets was much farther than standard ordnance from a one-fire mission. It meant Horne's reach was well beyond one thousand kilometers. It was a design that Enginsan Adelpa had been directly involved in himself, and one of the weapon advancements that resulted in the cornerstone of his wealth.

Most likely aimed at but not necessarily successful at targeting Ravagers, the trajectory of the launched rockets assured Nev that he was indeed heading in the right direction. He was closer than he thought. Something occurred to him, though. If *he* could see the trajectory of the rockets, he wondered if the Maulers could too.

More rockets shot past overhead, their wake shaking the sky they tore through, vibrating the ground beneath Nev's feet, and enveloping the area with the resounding thunder of their trajectory. This group had different coordinates. Maybe Horne had successfully located Ravager territory.

The fire missions looked like misses to Nev—a desperate scattershot. When the A-brid was heading to the dark mountains, it was a few klicks southeast from his current position.

He couldn't help but think how those rockets would be perceived by those they were intended for, and what they might do to counterattack.

Chapter 17

The cliffs jutted out and were so high that if they crumbled at the base, they would crush Fort Beckett when they collapsed. Thankfully, a different kind of movement caught Nev's eye, although probably more dangerous. He pulled out the binoculars he'd taken from the skiff to get a better look.

Outside the base was the runway where the pop-ship would be landing, but within the base, soldiers were mobilizing, equipment was being readied, and weapons were being stowed. It looked like a battalion was heading out soon. At least Horne had dropped steel rain first. Loading teams were busy reloading the Adelpa launchers. It looked like Tuhrelevim had more fire missions in its future.

Nev wanted to get to his wife, but sneaking into a military base was about as easy as dodging a bullet. Plus he was betting he wouldn't be welcomed after what had happened on the mission. Most likely Horne had concocted some story about him, something plausible with him supposedly dead. Even if he was able to get to Kate and both of them were able to get out of the base unscathed—which would be hopeless—where would they go? Where would they escape to? The dark mountains?

Unfortunately, it meant Nev needed to deal with who was on base first. That meant Horne. Just because he couldn't make it to his wife initially didn't mean he couldn't make it inside the base. He had to compartmentalize his mission, deal with one aspect at a time. Infiltrate the base first, and then decide the next priority.

There were cameras around the perimeter of the base and on top of the walls, but Nev knew of a shadow spot, where rock extended about a meter and could hide someone if they knew where it was. It was something another officer had mentioned offhand one time. Nev never knew he'd need to take advantage of it.

The great leaning cliffs looked much taller from within the confines of the base, and Nev stealthily followed their shadows. He waited for the guard to turn his head away for every inch he moved within Fort Beckett. If Nev moved slowly enough, he'd be able to get to the armory door before he was spotted by any fellow soldiers, most of whom he outranked. He knew that there were no guards posted on the inside.

Nev crept forward, keeping his eye on the guard, knowing that one sound could alert him and then Nev would have to deal with him. Either knock him out or kill him, and Nev didn't want to have to do either. Ordinarily he could pull rank on a subordinate, but Nev wasn't sure what the command was instructed to do if he showed up alive.

Once he was standing in front of the door, he punched in the numbers on the keypad, hoping the security code hadn't been changed in the few weeks he'd been away. Fortunately for him, the code still worked, and the mechanical door coughed open with a steely wheeze.

"Hey!"

Nev darted inside and punched the numbers on the keypad to the interior locking mechanism, a contingency he was exploiting. The soldier pounded on the door from the outside, yelling expletives, unaware of who had just broken into the armory. Knowing he would have nothing to worry about until he left its safety, Nev turned.

He whistled.

It was well stocked to say the least. Horne was gearing up for the next aspect of his mission, weapons Nev could have used for his own mission. He saw a familiar large case before him and smiled. Hopefully, he'd have use for the Shoulder Devils later. Now that he had weapons, Nev wouldn't have to kill the guard outside—he'd only have to knock him out. Nev wouldn't want him to spoil what he was quickly planning.

⅄

Makada was impatiently asking redundant questions, as he often did. Horne was used to it by now and never took it personally. Horne allowed it because Makada was the best. When someone has done a job for decades and obeyed the rules, Horne believed they deserved to bend those rules to suit them. It wasn't because of insecurity, quite the opposite actually. For Makada, questions—though at times pestering—allowed him to soak up every detail of a mission and sometimes a little more. He was searching for flaws and ways to improve upon it in ways that he may have missed in the introductory mission brief. Missions changed often, as any soldier who'd been in long enough knew.

Horne had no doubt Makada would soon attain the rank of colonel, probably faster than Horne had achieved it himself, and then quickly surpass it. Even though Horne respected Makada, the Major often tried his patience, and definitely Kayner's. He'd seen Kayner roll his eyes plenty of times today already. Horne had enough of the endless questioning today and changed the inflection of his responses, getting his irritation across. Makada always got the hint, but sometimes he'd still push a little more anyway. He was always looking for ways to get ahead, to strive to be the best, and to do his best, and he didn't really care how he went about making that happen.

Horne was just about to tell Makada to shut the fuck up when Captain Nev walked into the TOC aiming a Rovla assault rifle. The rest of the soldiers erupted and leapt up, grabbing and pointing their weapons, and Horne suddenly felt everything he'd been working on for years teetering.

"Whoa!" Kayner said, raising his hands. He motioned to the soldiers. "Stand down! Stand...down!"

"You're alive," Horne said.

Kayner looked over at Horne and then back to Nev. "And you look like you have something on your mind, sir." He turned to the soldiers. "Lower your weapons I said!" Then he refocused on Nev. "What do you need that for, sir?"

Nev's eyes brushed over the TOC. The soldiers had done as Sergeant Major Kayner had commanded. They still held their weapons at the ready, though.

Major Makada was as still as an Earth lion stalking prey.

"To get my point across," Nev said.

"And what point would that be, sir?" Kayner said.

"Colonel Horne is a traitor."

"Just calm down," Horne said.

"Shut your fucking mouth! My men are dead because of you!"

"That's preposterous!" Horne said. "We're in the *midst* of a mission! Our families, including yours, are in extreme danger until we secure this planet! Makada, get your men in here."

"Sir, don't you fucking move, or I'll cut you in half!"

It wasn't fear that flashed over Makada. What Nev had said pissed him off. He did as Nev said though and remained immobile. "You're only substantiating what you're accused of, Captain. You aren't acting like an innocent man."

Nev didn't know what Horne had fabricated about him, but it didn't matter. "Whatever he told you is a lie, sir."

Describing Makada as tough was putting it mildly. He had a strength about him that only elite soldiers possessed. He also had a quick-as-shit, lightning-fast temper; best just to stay out of his way—out of sight, out of mind. Technically overweight by military standards, he wasn't. His neck and other measurements didn't match because of how muscular he was. He wasn't a sprinter, but he surprised many leaner soldiers when he inexplicably passed them at the end of a PT run.

He looked at the world differently than most, kind of how large predatory cats on Earth did; they own it. It was also the way the world saw him. He stood out. He seemed to see everything without saying much, and when he did, he was usually asking questions—he always wanted to know everything—or chewing someone out. He was the kind of soldier who was at home on the battlefield, one meant to lead, and had all of the characteristics his enemies wouldn't want him to have.

He had dark hair and skin and blue eyes and was constantly being hit on by other soldiers' wives. He never did anything to encourage it and never reciprocated. He was married, but his wife had tipsily mentioned "mostly to the military." He would be polite to the women, wishing them a good day, and then corner their husbands later, annoyed by it. One story Nev had heard was about a soldier of low rank, new to the unit, and unfamiliar with Makada. Makada had told him his bitch was in heat and to keep her in line, and the soldier had told him to fuck off before spying his rank.

Makada had smoked him for an hour then taken away his weekend privileges so he could "participate" in extra duty. Nev didn't know if that story was true, but considering how much of an asshole Makada could be, especially to his subordinates, and how much he enjoyed it, the story probably wasn't too far off. Whenever Makada was brought up around soldiers with low rank, "Don't fuck with Makada" was usually the next thing out of their mouths.

"If you're with him," Nev said, nodding to Horne, "you're as guilty as him."

"He's not the one who has accusations against him," Makada said.

"He will."

"If anyone needs to disprove their guilt, it's you."

"You don't know what you're talking about, sir."

"Yet here you are, alone."

Makada was doing his best to get under Nev's skin. It was working. He tightened his grip on the Rovla.

"You fire that weapon," Kayner said, "and you'll have six hundred well-trained soldiers ordered to shoot you on sight, sir." Kayner spoke with a raspy growl. He'd been in the military for so long that it always sounded like he was losing his voice.

"Something tells me that's going to happen anyway," Nev said.

"That's not what we want," Kayner said.

"You want to kill more innocent people, Captain?" Horne said.

Nev opened his mouth to start yelling.

"You'll never see your wife again if you pull that trigger, son," Kayner said. "It'll make it that much worse for her. She thinks you're dead. We *all* did."

"Especially *him*," Nev said.

Horne stared back at him.

Kayner's hands were raised. "That's not for here and now."

They were allowing Kayner to control the conversation. Nev had the feeling he wasn't in on what had happened. Makada might not be either.

"He's lost his mind," Horne said. "We don't know where he's been or what he's gone through."

"Fucking liar," Nev said.

"Watch *your* mouth," Makada said.

Makada looked like a cobra about to strike. Nev looked over at Kayner. Both Kayner and Makada probably didn't know the truth. At this moment, it was Nev's word against Horne. That wasn't enough. This wasn't the way.

Horne honed in on that. "An immediate investigation will expose what went on out there, but that isn't going to happen here. It can't, not yet. Until then, why don't we pretend to be on the same side. You look shaken up."

Nev said nothing.

"Your disdain for me is obvious, but think of everyone else on this base. What's the enemy status?"

Nev said nothing. A colonel couldn't stop being a colonel, and Horne would do his best to extract information under any circumstances.

"He's right, sir," Kayner said to Nev. "Why don't you fill us in. We all have the time, until you consider putting down that weapon of yours. Let's let the past be the past for now, shall we?"

"All right," Nev lied. Part of being a soldier was selfless service so his own well-being wasn't important in the grand scheme of things. Especially considering what was out there.

Horne eyed him. "You saw something."

"What did you see?" Makada said, joining his compatriots.

"Beasts."

"Beasts are nothing new on Tuhrelevim," Makada said.

"Beasts...killing Ravagers." Nev saw a sharp spike of alarm, even in Makada.

"Are you sure whatever you saw weren't also Ravagers?" Horne said.

"Killing each other? No. The Maulers were smaller, more vicious, and coordinated. They had long tails. Ravagers don't have tails, and they moved faster. They were similar but definitely weren't Ravagers."

Silence filled the room.

"We hit them with artillery," Makada said, as if hoping that was enough.

"But you don't know the results of the mission," Nev said. "Isn't that why another battalion is being readied?" Nev looked over their faces. They gave away nothing. "Other than the Ravagers, we'll have this new threat to deal with if we stay here."

Horne let his confidence filter into his words. "We've got it under control."

"Ravagers are smarter than you think, I assure you, and you have this new predator to contend with."

"He's isn't telling us everything," Makada said.

Nev glared at him. "Why wouldn't I? We all have family here."

"I've been involved in enough interrogations to know when someone is hiding something."

That was true, but Makada was trying to rattle him. Nev didn't want to give any hint of what he was planning on doing. Even though he wasn't positive the Maulers were headed for Fort Beckett, he still had no plans to stay.

"Thank you for your warnings, Captain," Horne said. "But we don't know anything about this new type of beast you've claimed to see. Nimbus didn't mention them—"

"Exactly! Nimbus told me himself that very little of Tuhrelevim's life has been documented, that until—"

"Only *you* have seen them," Horne said, cutting him off. "We're very confident in our footing here. We *have to be* with the incoming population. And trust me, we've just wiped out *many* Ravagers. I can assure you of that."

Nev didn't let his anger show. Horne's arrogance was infuriating. "The incoming population will be killed if we stay here. We have no choice but to leave this planet."

"It can't be stopped," Horne said.

"Yes it can," Nev said. "And I'm going to stop it."

"They all know the risks and are willing to take those risks to come here."

"Keep telling yourself that."

Nev glanced over at Makada and saw that he'd snuck a hand on his pistol. Nev's initial plan was faltering. He might need these men. If he killed any of them in cold blood, there would be no way any other soldiers would help him, unless he could disguise his revenge somehow, some way he hadn't thought of yet. But Kate would be in danger. He couldn't let that happen. Revenge, especially against one man, maybe more, could wait.

He knew they were going to throw him in a cell, though. Even though the soldiers in the TOC could disarm him, he was sure there was a quick reaction force on their way to make that happen if they were somehow unable to. So when he heard them mobilize behind him, he wasn't surprised.

"Drop the weapon!" one of them yelled.

Makada had a satisfied smirk on his face.

Nev lowered the Rovla and set it on the floor. "How long will I be held for?"

"Until the investigation of your mission is complete," Horne said.

Nev's hands were zip-tied behind his back. "Will someone please inform my wife I'm still alive?"

Chapter 18

Nev received looks on his way to the stockade as if he were a traitor. The soldiers must have been briefed along those lines since his arrival. The soldier who escorted him, Private Jones, had held the rank of specialist before Nev had approved his demotion. Jones and a few others had decided to go outside the wire without approval. It was only to see more of the world they were stationed on, but Tuhrelevim was extremely dangerous and needless risk of personnel was unacceptable. Nev understood, though. Grunts weren't often needed for much else than their main job, and sometimes that job wasn't particularly eventful and could even be boring, like guard duty. There was a lot to see on Tuhrelevim, but unfortunately for most of the soldiers, what they saw was only from within the protective walls of the base during their morning PT run.

The stockade was about the size of a warehouse. It had multiple cells and was all electronically operated, its power from stored solar energy. If every human left tomorrow, Fort Beckett would run on its own for years. With so much space available on the planet, humans were wasting no time expanding and taking up as much room as they liked. The stockade could have held a battalion of soldiers. Nev hadn't paid much attention before now; only when he was a prisoner himself did he begin to wonder why.

There was part of Nev that knew he'd be arrested after walking into the TOC. Wanted to be, even, because the stockade was probably the safest place to strategize, knowing what was likely incoming. He'd wanted to kill Horne, but he wouldn't have, not in the TOC anyway, and now he was being punished with silence, no matter how many demands he made of Jones.

Nev missed Kate and the stress-free days of their life together, when there wasn't a mission right around the corner. He needed some R and R with her badly, but as he'd done his entire career, he relied on his training. He had no choice other than to deal with where he was. Patience was practically a muscle every soldier could flex when they needed to. He was used to having to hurry up and wait, except Kate was waiting for *him*.

He couldn't think of that now. Focusing on and executing each parameter of the mission was the strength and foundation of being a soldier, and that was exactly what he would do. But while he was here, he might as well do his best to extract as much information as possible. All he had was time, and he'd try to use every second to his advantage.

Jones sat in front of Nev's cell staring straight ahead, right through him, practically through the wall, a penetrating stare that most soldiers learned in basic training. It was a frame of mind that could go undisturbed by whoever tried to break their concentration. Nev wondered how long it would take Jones to crack as he continued to reiterate what he'd been saying since he'd been put in the cell.

"I need to get a message to my wife."

Jones said nothing.

"Think of it like this, would you want to be treated this way if you had my rank? Hey, Private, did you hear me?"

"Yeah, Nev. I did."

A response. It was disrespectful, but at least it was a start. Although a subordinate calling a superior by their last name only, negating their rank, meant Jones expected Nev to get demoted. As if he was already pronounced guilty of whatever he was suspected of doing. *Prick.*

"Whatever it is that they say I've done, I didn't do, and if you don't help me I'm going to make sure you never reach the rank of specialist again."

Jones turned red and faked a confident smile. "Shut up, Nev. Never liked you."

"Then I did my job, and you're a better soldier for it. You aren't supposed to like me. You still see the rank on my uniform, right Jones?"

That made him straighten up. Ironically, superiors could refer to soldiers by their last name only.

"You seem to be under the impression that I'm guilty of whatever the fuck they told you. What is it they think I did?"

Horne. Un-fucking-believable. It took a while for Jones to tell him more, but after some more baiting, Nev learned Horne had briefed the entire base that Nev had killed his entire squad, including Nimbus, due to stress from encountering the Ravagers, and then had been killed by the predators. When he showed up alive, Nev hoped doubt about those accusations would be raised, and he could eventually rally his fellow soldiers to testify to his character. He also learned that Lieutenant Colonel Pritchard was sent out with his battalion and were still "missing." They were probably all dead, if they had faced the Ravagers.

Fort Beckett was Horne's baby. Nimbus had told Nev as much. Horne had conceived, designed, and overseen its construction and would clearly do anything he had to in order for Operation Tuhrelevim to be a success. Pritchard and Horne had been good friends. If he'd send his friends to their deaths, then there was nothing he wouldn't do. Another battalion being sent out was a huge mistake. Even if they were mobile enough to attack and then retreat back to base, Tuhrelevim held too many secrets.

"I'm innocent, kid."

"Your guilt or innocence will be determined by your trial."

"There won't be a trial, dipshit. We'll all be dead by then. I need to talk to Lieutenant Colonel Mathis."

"You won't be talking to anybody while you're in there."

Nev thought of Kate and how distraught she must be because of the allegations. "And how long do you think I'll be in here?"

Private Jones turned to stone again.

Nev needed to talk to somebody—other than Horne, or Makada, or Kayner—somebody who would listen, to warn them of how dangerous it was to stay on this planet. It sure as hell wasn't going to be Jones. Nev had always respected Mathis and decided he needed to speak with him immediately. No doubt Mathis and his men would be deployed soon.

"Private, I didn't do what they're saying I did, but you'll learn that soon enough. I've been through a lot. I was betrayed, and because of that, my men got killed. Good men. Good soldiers. I'm sure you knew them or at least knew *of* them. I need a message passed to Lieutenant Colonel Mathis. I need to speak with him so more good men don't get killed. I'm not asking to leave this cell. All I'm asking you to do is pass the message. That's all. Please."

"You're right. I did know them. Can't help you…Nev."

"You fucking little shit! Damn it!"

Jones smiled then, pleased with himself. Nev wondered how long he'd smile if one of those predators ate his guts while he was still alive to see it.

Nev closed his eyes, exhaling, allowing his anger and frustration to dissipate. He didn't want that, even though Jones deserved it. They needed all able-bodied soldiers on this base—even a shit-bag like Jones, who wore that shit-eating grin of his like a badge of honor.

Nev knew he'd never escape. The stockade was guarded too well, electronically operated with state of the art technology, and manned by soldiers determined to keep him there. There was nothing else he could do so he decided to get some rest.

Until Nev heard an explosion outside that rocked the base so hard that the reinforced floor rattled beneath their feet. Jones had stood up, a terrified look on his face. He had probably been taking a nap.

"Get on the radio and find out what's happening!" Nev ordered.

Jones looked at him, wide-eyed. The shouts of the soldiers outside could be heard even through the reinforced steel walls.

"Just stay calm," Jones said, taking deep, panicky breaths.

"I am calm. What the fuck are you doing, soldier? Forget what's going on in here. It's out there you need to worry about now!"

"Shut the fuck up!"

Nev felt his anger return. "You should have listened to me."

Chapter 19

Prowling shadows stalked Fort Beckett. Speed seemed to be their strategy. They didn't want to reveal themselves where Ravagers weren't afraid to do so. Soldiers saw glimpses, blurs of speed, but weren't able to target them accurately. There was talk over the net about what they were, that they were Ravagers, but those who had seen Ravagers before broke through net traffic and corrected them. They were something new, what the prisoner, Captain Nev had described, and they were quickly infiltrating Fort Beckett, figuring things out.

There were suddenly reports over the net by soldiers who got a clear look at them, as if the Maulers collectively decided to reveal themselves. They were bigger than a large dog but smaller than a Ravager and silent, stealthier, and more feline in their movements. There was a report—supposedly from a soldier who had seen them, but nobody knew who or how—that they were smarter than Ravagers. The ones who were able to get a message over the net had most likely been killed. Seconds after contacting higher, their radio silence was proof of that, as if they'd been targeted.

The screams were suddenly everywhere. The Maulers had obviously concluded that they'd spent enough time reconning the base.

Squads were pummeled by Maulers that launched themselves from rooftops, landing in the middle of them. Entire platoons suddenly found themselves down to one or two soldiers and then only one soldier, who ran for his life before he was tackled.

Blood splattered over a group, and only then would they realize that one of them was on the ground, clawed open. They raised their weapons and fired.

A soldier scanned the distance looking for the source of what was attacking them, trying to block out the frenzied chaos that had erupted. Movement caught his eye in a puddle in front of his boot. The thing in the reflection dropped, causing the puddle to explode, and covered the soldier's boots with his own blood.

He found himself on his back and watched with horror as the beast drove its jaws into his stomach. There was no training to endure that kind of pain. He screamed.

⅄

A soldier was screaming over the net, heard by the stunned personnel of the TOC. It sounded like he was being ripped limb from limb. The mic must have still been activated. Any soldier who sent a report over the net was silent after and didn't respond when hopeless attempts of radio contact were made by the RTOs.

Horne, Makada, Kayner, and the rest of the men were on their feet, listening intently, silently waiting for confirmation or more information about this new enemy. Instead, there was only the aggravating silence of an empty radio net.

Horne looked to Makada.

⅄

Three A-brids ascended over Fort Beckett like confident insects looking for easy prey, the gyrations of their blades blasting noise together, the chop of them flying overhead resounded over the base. They flew in tandem, ready to end the threat.

As the hybrid jet/helicopters began taking out targets, radio chatter picked up again, the fight turning back in human favor. The Maulers tracking the aircraft above them opened them up to the soldiers on the ground.

As the radio chatter ramped up, so did the audible weapons fire in the background, when seconds before there had only been death or deathly silence. It was a relief to hear that so many soldiers were still alive. Murmurs of confidence began to spread again throughout the TOC, and the men resumed their jobs, no longer still as statues while listening to horrors they could not stop. Except for Horne. He didn't budge. His angry expression immovable from his face.

"Adelpa-two pilots standing by, sir," Makada said.

"Allow the A-brids to chew those fuckers up first," Horne said. "Then the Adelpa twos will make them wish they'd never laid a fucking paw inside Fort Beckett."

"Yes, sir."

Multiple RTOs belted their superiors' orders over the net. Now it was their turn.

⅄

Soldiers were able to coordinate and form lines of fire against the Maulers. The A-brids made multiple passes, and the strapped-in soldiers fired twenty-millimeter chain guns, continuously pelting the four-legged intruders.

It was working. The Maulers were falling back, practically scrambling to get their legs moving fast enough to get themselves out of the base. They obviously weren't prepared for the aircraft.

The TOC was informed of the progress, reports of soldiers firing at the haunches of fleeing Maulers. Now that they knew what they were up against, the men were able to form squads again, shooting simultaneously to drop the enemy. They hooted and hollered in victory as the Maulers galloped away, leaving even faster than they'd infiltrated.

A-brids continued to drive the Maulers out. Not just the ones still trying to scramble out of the base, but the ones outside it too.

⅄

The communication between the A-brid pilots and the TOC was constant.

"Maulers still within walls of base, break...Maulers outside base heading north, break...Maulers climbing the cliff faces. We've got them on the run! How copy, over?"

A slight smile finally broke through the anger on Horne's face, and quiet cheers of victory sounded among the soldiers.

Makada pressed the mic. "Good copy. Take out as many as you can, over."

"Wilco."

Kayner put a fresh stick of gum in his mouth as he threw on his flak vest. He wasn't as quick to celebrate. NCOs were smart not to. He pushed a clip into his pistol and pulled the slide back before holstering the weapon. Even the grunts grew cautious. Let the officers pat each other on the back and celebrate before the battle was won.

⅄

The Maulers had split up and climbed up the steep, craggy cliffs that surrounded the base as if they were born to them. Their short powerful legs and long claws allowed them to do it quickly. What would be precarious for a human gave the Maulers grip.

The three A-brids ascended and followed, firing and killing the scrambling beasts easily. If the hundreds of rounds per second didn't kill them, then most likely the fall would—hard to keep grip, with hundreds of bullets tearing up their flesh.

The Maulers were excellent climbers though, and they'd already climbed hundreds of feet. Fort Beckett was beginning to look like a miniature version of itself below.

The three A-brids were carefully spaced, two facing west and the other facing east. The booming chain guns pelted the cliffs on both sides, and climbing Maulers fell constantly. The TOC hadn't warned them of how many Maulers there would be. Perhaps they didn't know. Their attack had happened so suddenly.

Suddenly one of the A-brids rocked violently and was sent reeling. Something had hit it, but before the pilot could do anything about it or communicate what he'd seen, the aircraft crashed into the cliffside and exploded.

The heat of the blast made the gunner of the closest A-brid turn away. "What happened?"

"Was that ordnance?" the pilot said.

"Negative," the gunner said. "Nothing came from below."

He looked up; something blotted out the sun, getting bigger, closer—something falling. It looked like…

The pilot of the other A-brid saw something crash through the blades of the A-brid before them, shredded instantly, leaving only red mist. The damage it caused was catastrophic, as if the aircraft had been hit with a missile.

Alarms blared as it rocked back and forth and shook. Black smoke billowed thickly from the rotor, the rotating blades blasting it everywhere and then engulfing the aircraft, obscuring it from view. Then the A-brid was falling out of the sky.

The pilot of the remaining A-brid pulled the stick hard to the right, flying away from the cliffs, away from the trap they'd been led into. Not fast enough, though. A Ravager landed heavily on the side of the A-brid, missing its mark. It was aiming for the blades like the previous two had, to sacrifice itself and take out the aircraft.

The fact that the pilot had moved and disrupted its mission seemed to anger it. The huge beast was now roaring into the interior, striking at the gunner with its massive claws. The weight of it sent the A-brid into a spin, and the pilot turned to see the gunner in the Ravager's mouth. Blood flew everywhere as it crunched the man between its teeth and then tried to force its massive body inside to get at the pilot.

Its weight made it impossible for the pilot to regain control, and seconds after, the A-brid hit the side of the cliff.

⅄

Through the TOC windows they could see the explosion in the distance and felt its muffled vibration.

"What the *hell* just happened?" Horne bellowed, looking around for answers, seeing none.

"We've lost the A-brids, sir."

"No shit!"

"What's our next move, sir?" Makada said.

"Get those Adelpas in the air."

"Yes, sir," Makada said. "You heard him."

The RTO grabbed the mic, relaying the order. He spun toward Makada. "Sir, the Adelpa pilots are reporting they're unable to reach the aircraft."

"Why the fuck not?" Horne said.

The RTO hesitated.

"Private, relay that information!" Makada said.

"What they're saying doesn't make sense, sir. They sound confused."

"Of course they're fucking confused," Makada said. "Say it anyway!"

"Ravagers have joined the Maulers in the attack."

Horne turned a deep red. "*What?*"

Chapter 20

Nev was out of earshot of net traffic, but he knew what was happening. The guards panicked and prepared as if the battle outside would soon be inside. They faced the door, unrealistically waiting for the beasts to figure out the electronically operated door and its twelve-digit code to activate the locking mechanism. Even Jones faced outward, away from Nev who simply sat, plotted, and waited.

Then the unthinkable happened: the entrance door to the stockade actually opened. A soldier rushed in, a desperate illogical attempt to survive, and then tried to shut the door behind him. A Mauler barreled through.

The electronically operated door was wrenched open, and terrified men ran across Nev's eye line. Jones abandoned his post, and the stockade erupted with weapons fire, deafening in the close quarters. Nev saw three Maulers, just like the ones he'd seen killing Ravagers. If they could get into an electronically operated state of the art stockade, they could go anywhere in Fort Beckett. Nev thought of Kate. He *had* to get the hell out of here.

Barking snarls and growls audibly mixed with gunfire, and the floor began to bleed as human bodies fell. The forward attack by the soldiers turned into a retreat as they died one after the other. They fired as they ran in all directions. The Maulers killed any man they got their teeth and claws into and did it quick, like they had it planned that way. As if they had a mission of their own.

Nev could only watch the soldiers fight for their lives and the Maulers kill them. He had no way to help them. The soldiers concentrated fire on one and were able to kill it, and then they hobbled another's legs, giving them a chance to shoot it in the head. That left one more, but the soldiers had accidentally bunched up, and the Mauler barreled into them, knocking them to the ground. The men had no chance without their weapons aimed, and the Mauler took lightning-fast swipes with its razor-sharp claws, plunging into their stomachs. Gore erupted as if the men had exploded.

The Mauler turned, covered in blood. Jones was trembling, pretending to be dead like a coward. His slight movement was inescapable to the Mauler's keen senses, and it charged him. Jones leapt up and ran at Nev's cell, inexplicably pleading for him to let him in. There was nothing Nev could do for the young man. The Mauler tackled him against the steel bars, crushing him and then mauling him horribly.

Nev took a step back when Jones's blood sprayed. He wondered what he could have possibly been thinking. Panic had made Jones head for a locked door, instead of the open stockade door. Nev hadn't forgotten that door for a moment.

Bloody faced, the Mauler raised its yellow eyes and looked directly at him. Nev could actually sense its hatred. It knew he was its enemy. It let out a low, muffled wet growl as Jones's blood still dripped from its mouth, and it vibrated with each angry breath.

It had a snubbed face—unlike the pronounced muzzle of a Ravager—and extremely large fangs for its mouth. It was smaller than a Ravager too; squatter, wider, with more muscle, and had stripes like a Ravager but not the same pattern. Its well-muscled body looked like it was made for taking prey down to the ground before killing it. Nev already knew they were pack hunters.

Jones's Rovla assault rifle was in between the bars. The Mauler's eyes narrowed, locked on Nev as it contemplated its own plan of attack, its tail the only part of it that moved. It thrashed on its own, seemingly unaware of the brain that controlled it, giving away its impatient bloodthirsty intentions. It wanted to kill Nev and then move on to hunt down the next human.

If Nev moved slowly enough, maybe he could grab the weapon before the Mauler got hold of his arm. He reached forward about an inch, and the Mauler curled its lips back, exposing more of its massive teeth, a low snarl escaping the back of its throat. Before Nev could act, the Mauler launched itself at the bars; the extreme force of the impact actually bent the steel.

Nev stepped back, and his legs hit the bunk, unable to get any farther away from the beast as it growled and snarled and spit ferociously, struggling to get in at him, pushing with its head and pulling at the bars at the same time. The Mauler's head began to squeeze through.

"Holy *shiiit!*"

It reared back and sprung forward again, with even more force this time, pulling at the bars with its massive, muscular paws and driving forward with its powerful legs. The bars spread farther, enough for the Mauler to push forward with all its strength and begin to work its entire head into the cell.

It was going to get in—Nev was reminded of an Earth rat squeezing through an opening the size of a dime. No wonder they'd been able to infiltrate the base. Nev bet their point of entry hadn't even been determined yet.

Nev quickly dropped, reached out, and grabbed the butt of the weapon. The Mauler stomped on the barrel, but Nev yanked hard, and it slipped out from under its wide paw. The Mauler leaned back on its muscular haunches, ready to spring forward.

Nev aimed the weapon at its head. The Mauler growled angrily and moved left and then quickly right, as if it was aware of what the weapon could do. Nev anticipated another dodge and fired into its face, blasting bullets into the Mauler's eyes, the weapon fire splashing blinding light into the dim cell.

The Mauler tried to back away but not before Nev was able to empty the rest of the clip into it. The bullets must have caused serious trauma to its brain because its back legs stopped working, and it was unable to back itself out of the cell it was now stuck in. The Mauler collapsed and bled out, a grimace of pain on its face. Its front legs worked in a stutter, a slow kick until it didn't move anymore.

Above it, over its back, it looked like there was enough room for Nev to squeeze through. Unfortunately, he'd have to climb over the top of it. He truly hoped it was dead. He approached slowly, aiming the Rovla, looking for any hint that it was still alive.

Jones's body was under the Mauler. The soldier's corpse was mangled horribly. With him and the Mauler dead, a lake of blood had formed in the cell, making each step precarious. Nev didn't want to slip and fall head first, especially if the thing turned out to still be alive. The gunfire and shouting and chaos could be heard outside, though no more Maulers had entered the stockade. It was as if only a small squad of them had been sent in.

Nev stepped to the Mauler's side. He reached out with the weapon and tapped it with the barrel. No reaction. No movement. Nothing.

He slung the Rovla around his back. Reaching up, he put an arm over the top of it. The Mauler was so muscular that it felt like he was grasping warm steel. He pulled himself up, barely squeezing himself through the small opening, and then over the Mauler, landing on the red floor.

Nev knew he'd end up covered in blood, and he was. He carefully got to his feet and ran for the door, risking a glance behind him.

The Mauler hadn't moved.

It was dead, but the encounter still gave Nev chills from head to toe.

Chapter 21

"Captain Nev was wrong," Makada said. "The Maulers and Ravagers aren't enemies."

The extremity of the error was apparent, especially for Horne. The transmissions to the TOC said as much, reporting multiple engagements with both Maulers and Ravagers fighting together. Captain Nev may have concocted the story he'd told them before he'd been taken to the stockade, except Horne knew Captain Nev better than that. He was honorable and must have been mistaken somehow.

Because the attack had commenced so swiftly and many of the beasts were already within the perimeter of the base, those watching the cameras had probably initially incorrectly identified the Maulers as Ravagers.

And now most of the cameras weren't operational, most likely destroyed, except for a few, as if the beasts wanted to control the soldiers' attention. At least that was the opinion of a few of the TOC personnel.

Makada's arms flexed involuntarily at his sides. "The Maulers drew the A-brids to the cliffs pretending to flee, sacrificing themselves, but drawing them in, and because the A-brids hardly had to move, they were set up neatly as direct targets for the Ravagers to take down."

"Once the A-brids were down, the Maulers turned back and resumed their attack within the base," Kayner said. "They were only feigning defeat."

"Then the Ravagers could get to the aircraft that wasn't airborne," Horne said quietly. "Quite cunning."

Makada and Kayner flashed glances.

"We are under attack!"

The desperation in the soldier's voice snapped their attention back into focus. Horne's temper flared. "We gonna do something about that?"

"There aren't as many soldiers at that north side," Kayner said. "Most are still engaging the Maulers at the west."

"We need to get them there," Horne bellowed.

Makada quickly surveyed the TOC. "Sir, permission to join the fight?"

"Granted."

Makada smiled.

"Wait, which one?" Horne said.

"I'll start at the north side, sir. I'll need three soldiers."

"You got 'em. Go."

Makada pointed, and the three soldiers he'd already planned on taking along left with him.

"I'd like to go too, sir," Kayner said.

"Negative, Sergeant Major," Horne said. "I want your priority to be the TOC."

"All due respect, sir, with what's going on out there, there soon won't be a TOC to prioritize. You still have Mathis."

"You talk like you won't be coming back."

"Do what I got to do, sir. My men are dying right now. I'm no better than them."

Horne considered it, weighing that and all of the other things he had to contend with.

"*Come on*, sir," Kayner said, pushing the way only a sergeant major could. "At least let me go out there to motivate the men. Keep them afraid of me. They'll fight better for it. Besides, we both know the Major's coming back."

Horne smiled and then nodded.

"Thank you, sir."

Horne understood. The TOC was no place for a man like Kayner even though Horne wanted him there. Like Makada, his place was the battlefield. Just like all the other soldiers in the TOC.

"In fact, all of you go with the Sergeant Major," Horne said. "I can handle the fucking radios. Go, men! Now!"

They leapt up and threw on their gear as fast as they could. Kayner spit his gum out and put in a fresh piece. He put on his full battle rattle, somehow doing it faster than all of the young soldiers who did the same around him, grabbed a Rovla, and then they all headed out.

⅄

The first thing Kayner did was target a lone Mauler sniffing around just outside the TOC. It was a good thing he'd volunteered to go out. Horne sure as hell didn't need one of those things getting inside. Saying Horne was vital to the mission was an understatement. The whole thing hinged on him.

The striped beast saw him and snarled, but half a clip from Kayner's Rovla put it down. He glanced up, scanned for other soldiers, keeping his eyes on the Mauler in case it wasn't dead, looking for men to command. There were stragglers everywhere—one- and two-man battle-buddy teams. That wouldn't do.

"Hey!" Kayner yelled with a voice hoarse from nearly thirty years of yelling at soldiers. "Group up, damn it!"

A staff sergeant nodded and barked orders into his shoulder radio as one of his men covered him. Other stragglers arrived at their position. They'd formed enough to defend their perimeter, just over a squad.

When enough soldiers had amassed at Kayner's position, now just over a platoon's worth, he addressed the group. Communication between soldiers was different under battle conditions. Typically those in charge would have taken those with lesser rank aside, communicated what needed to be done, and then their NCOs would have delegated to the soldiers under them. This wasn't one of those times.

"We're going to make a push to the other side of the base," Kayner shouted. "Join our fellow soldiers in the thick of it where most of those beasts are. They're trying to reduce our airpower. We can't let that happen."

The soldiers watched Kayner intently, thankful he'd taken charge and compartmentalized the mission for them, prioritized the fighting. It was what most soldiers needed, an objective, no matter how big or small. It allowed them to be their best.

"You, you, and you, watch our six. Let's move!"

"Yes, Sergeant Major!"

Kayner aimed at the far end of the base. His shots weren't accurate with a silencer attached, but his intent wasn't to kill the beasts. They were too far away, unless he got a lucky shot. It was to keep the enemy off the soldiers' asses, let the creatures know they'd been seen, and limit the possibility they could take down one of his soldiers as the platoon moved.

⅄

The constant weapons fire was mostly by Rovlas, even though there were SDs, but there weren't many of those. Not all soldiers would have used a Shoulder Devil anyway. Many were monogamous to one weapon system, no matter how powerful an alternative one was. Most preferred Rovlas because they were more comfortable with them and had spent their military careers firing them. SDs required much more skill and training.

The Ravagers had smashed up the Adelpa aircraft before they'd even been started up, destroying them and leveling the battlefield. Soldiers fired in all directions as both kinds of beasts continued to stream in. There were so many of them. They were winning.

Until Makada got into the fight, armed with two M331a2 weapon systems. For Makada, the SDs were perfect.

"Clear a path for Makada!" an officer commanded.

Soldiers shouted the command to one another, and it echoed from squad to squad and across the net. Not just because of his rank, but because his strategies required such awareness, skill, and technique that if it all didn't happen perfectly, soldiers could get themselves killed. It was a tactic they'd trained for over and over again at Makada's insistence and was his biggest contribution to Operation Tuhrelevim thus far.

They spotted him, pointed, and fired at the edges of the battle, pushing the beasts back. Makada and his squad were on the run. Two Devils hovered over his shoulders, and his squad held Rovlas. Soldiers respondent to the net command handling the threat momentarily were trusted to create a path wide enough for him and his squad to get through. They fired at the outer perimeter. Grenades exploded deep into the beasts, allowing Makada and his squad to cover considerable ground.

Makada's intent wasn't to protect the Adelpa aircraft. He already knew they were destroyed. It was simply to kill as many of the enemy as possible. And a lot was possible because the beasts were pouring in from that side of the base. Makada never slowed as he fired—him and his entire squad. The soldiers had created space before the destroyed wall as they'd hoped—the enemy entrance point—giving them ample firing room. Makada targeted the open-mouthed beasts that clawed forward, the end of the group couldn't even be spotted. Ravagers and Maulers mixed, difficult to tell which beast was in charge, or if that trait was even a variable.

Makada's squad of three soldiers protected him, firing at, hobbling, and sometimes killing the beasts that tried to get to him. That way Makada could keep up his running speed and take out as many of them as he could. The SDs obeyed their operator, forced to rise, fall, and whip around to spray bullets. It looked as if he were only pointing with the SD controllers, but that simple motion resulted in spurting blood, exploding gore, and death to the beasts that tried their best to get to him, linked to his target placement that ground forth with powerful, unstoppable metal death.

Makada targeted multiple groups of the beasts at once and was able to slow and then halt their infiltration. The barrage of bullets were like invisible punches that killed them in his line of fire, knocking them back. The SDs required training and natural skill, and Makada possessed them both, he used them like a master, as if he'd invented Shoulder Devils himself. It allowed other soldiers to squeeze and condense their sectors of fire, to get the battle under their control, all the while commands were sent over the net.

With Makada's support, the soldiers were able to push forward where most of the beasts were getting through. The battle shifted more in the humans' favor with every step, and soon no more Ravagers or Maulers were entering. They only had to fight the ones alive and still inside the base. Maybe it was the last of them?

Suddenly hundreds of Ravagers fought to get in—through the opening, appearing up high on the rooftops and jumping down. They vaulted over the wall. Now there were just as many of them as before. The soldiers had been baited. They faced a high wall of fierce long teeth and eyes that reflected their weapons fire, hoping to close in on them. Makada slowed and then stopped with his squad, looking for another point of attack.

Then the beasts made another push from the broken wall, and, like a dam cracking, it burst, spilling forth even more of them. The beasts were not concerned with their own lives. Their objective was to invade and kill, and they were willing to die to do that.

Makada ended up on his back, his squad already bloodied and screaming or dead or dying. He fired his Shoulder Devils at the approaching enemy, the report echoing, suddenly his were the only weapons shooting, the muzzle flashes almost obscuring the many snarling Ravagers and Maulers before him, intent on tearing him apart.

Chapter 22

Nev's breath caught as the battle swirled around him. He couldn't believe what he was seeing: Maulers and Ravagers, fighting together. It should have been all Ravagers, or all Maulers, but no. What he'd witnessed on his way back to Fort Beckett must have been a fluke, something rare that he didn't understand. There would be time to study their behavior later, but now was not that time. All that mattered was Kate.

The battle had drawn most of the beasts to the center of the base, and Nev recognized Kayner commanding soldiers. Even at this distance, Kayner's age made him stand out, and not in a good way. He was around fifty. Not old for a civilian but ancient for the military. His mind was able, but his body wasn't capable of what that mind demanded of it, and he fell short in too many aspects, even before they got to him.

The soldiers around him did their best to prevent it, desperate to keep him alive, and they fought hard to do so. Kayner was surely the driving force of their fight, and without him his subordinates would be completely lost—at least temporarily—but in those seconds more susceptible to attack. There was nothing they could do.

Nor was there anything Nev could do. He didn't have a radio and was too far away to warn him of the Ravager that stalked him from behind.

⅄

Horne was at the radio, probably trying to send more reinforcements, though Nev couldn't hear him. When he'd seen Kayner die, the first thing Nev thought of was that they needed more soldiers, but then he'd remembered why he'd come back in the first place. For Kate.

Nev raised a pistol. "Did you honestly think I'd forget what you did, sir?"

Horne looked over at him, obvious that his plan was crumbling. "You were wrong about the Maulers."

"Where is everyone?"

"Sent them out."

"Haven't you got enough men killed?"

"You twist the truth."

"And what would that be?"

"The purpose behind the things I've done."

"I have an idea."

"We owe humanity."

"We serve humanity. We owe nothing. Least of all to a society *you* plan on creating."

Horne still held the mic, still held the power—couldn't have that.

"Put that mic down, sir," Nev said. "You've done enough damage. Sacrificed enough lives."

"Sacrificed, yes. For their families. For my grandchildren and maybe even yours."

"You want your grandchildren to live *here*?"

Horne paused. "At some point, yes. Provide a home for them. For all of us."

"A home or a vacation destination?"

"I don't know what Nimbus told you…living isn't just about surviving, scraping by, it's also about enjoying."

"I know what life is about."

"Do you? Are you sure? A life in the military is hardly a life at all. How much time have you spent with your wife, Captain? Or have you been *in* too long to know how dysfunctional all of this is?" Horne glanced down at the pistol. "You sure you want to do that? It's wasting time."

Nev tightened his grip on the weapon. "Are you trying to get more soldiers down here?"

"We're at war. Of course I am!"

"Your war."

"This planet will be another home for humanity."

"Who are you to decide that? Why this planet? It could be any of them."

"You mean all those lifeless rocks in the dark? Something about this one speaks to me. I'm sure even you sense it. It reminds me of Earth."

"No shit! But by inhabiting it the indigenous species will die, just as they did on Earth."

"But humans will live on."

"At the expense of other life."

"Superior life."

"Hardly. They're a lot like us."

"Which, the Mauler or the Ravager?"

"That's precisely my point. You don't know enough. You didn't even know about the Maulers until I told you about them."

"Intelligence like ours can't exist on four legs."

"Don't be a fool. Have you ever looked one of them in the eyes? I have. The Ravagers are essentially human in terms of intelligence. What me and my men encountered were only their recon, their scouts, and don't compare to what they've sent at us now. We're fighting their army—"

"Listen to you. I understand your fear—"

"Of course I'm afraid!" Nev said. "I'm afraid that no one will leave this planet alive, and you should be, too."

"Killing is a moral conundrum, we both know that, but which side are you on, Captain?"

"It isn't about sides."

"Who are you to stop me? Let me ask you that. What you're implying would halt human exploration—our natural trajectory. There's too much momentum. We are biologically driven to spread, especially to this planet. It's so much like Earth."

"Except it isn't."

"It's the closest thing. All the depression, the suicides, all of it can be avoided if we move here."

"It's not Earth, damn it! And if we stay everyone will die. We're outmatched. Put that mic down, sir."

Horne ignored him. "You kill me, you kill humanity. Maybe not today, or in a hundred years, but eventually." Horne looked past Nev, raised his hands, and began walking toward him. "I'm sorry about what happened out there. They weren't just your men, but men die in war. I shouldn't have to remind you of that. We're fighting for our survival!"

Nev shot Colonel Horne in the left eye, blowing out the back of his head. He was killed instantly. He was a big man, and he went down hard, falling into the table that supported the radios, and all of it tipping over with a crash much louder than Nev wanted.

Horne's body lay over the equipment. His large hand still held the mic.

"Captain Nev, drop the weapon!"

Nev spun to see Makada, who had a Shoulder Devil controller aimed at him. The M331a2 weapon system peeked over his shoulder, hovering, ready to unleash death. Nev hadn't noticed he was there until he'd spoken. Makada was covered in blood. Whose blood Nev couldn't be sure, but the fact that he was still on his feet probably meant it wasn't his.

"What happened to the other soldiers, sir?" Nev said.

"Fighting or dead or dying."

"You abandoned them." It wasn't a question.

"Horne ordered me back."

"So you say."

"After I volunteered to go out. Captain, drop that weapon. I'm not going to say it again."

Reasoning with Makada would be pointless. He was smart enough to understand the things Nev had done, but he wouldn't care. He'd been in the military for too long, was too brainwashed. Aside from the facts that Nev had just executed his superior and that Nev and Makada had detested each other ever since they'd met, Makada was the type to obey orders and uphold the chain of command at any cost.

Then again, Nev wondered how long Makada had been standing there before he'd shot Horne. Maybe that was why Horne had walked toward him, thinking Makada would step in, and Makada hadn't acted fast enough. Or maybe he'd waited on purpose, hoping for what happened to happen so he could take Horne's place. Not many rules out here in space. The soldier with the highest rank was in charge.

All this wondering why wasn't going to stop the threat of him. Makada could have already painted a target line over Nev. If he had, it didn't matter what Nev did, the SD would deploy to eliminate him. His only chance of survival was if Makada hadn't done that already. Nev wheeled, still clutching the pistol, and with the other hand threw a field manual at Makada's head, causing him to shield his eyes and raise the SD controller upright. The Shoulder Devil crashed into the ceiling, giving Nev the few seconds he needed to break into a run.

Makada's SD whined its three-second delay, and then churning firepower boomed. Nev could feel the reverberation of the weapon against his back—midair—and thought he'd been shot. He went over Horne's desk, and it exploded behind him, covering him in sharp little bits as he hit the floor, the impact of the fall forcing him to drop the pistol. The desk had just saved his life. It was made from the thick wood of Tuhrelevim's trees, ones Nev didn't know the name of. Oak-like, but not. Thankfully the SD clicked empty, and Nev suddenly had a chance.

Until Makada tackled him.

The fight had just begun, and Nev was already on the ground, losing. When he and Makada had met, Nev remembered thinking that Makada was the type you hoped you never had to fight. Not just because he was strong physically, but mentally too. He had a way about him that almost made you feel sorry for his enemies.

Nev had been right. Makada struck him with elbows and knees and fists that really fucking hurt, able to slip in and deliver blows the way only someone who had natural fighting skills could.

The two tumbled about the office, invisible to the battle going on outside it because of the fog windows that were impossible to see through in either direction. Nev was able to get on his feet, but then he somehow felt his lower lip split and pain in his ribs at the same time. At least it felt that way. Makada was that fast. Then he was back on the ground, again, struggling to escape Makada's holds and bends and near-breaks.

Nev was outmatched in every sense. Still being sore from fighting Nimbus on the A-brid wasn't helping. Not that it would have mattered. Makada was so focused on beating Nev to death that he didn't realize Nev had got a hold of the pistol again. Nev put it to Makada's head, but Makada quickly chopped upward, and the weapon blasted the ceiling.

Taking advantage of the shock from firing the weapon, Nev jumped up, still holding the pistol, but Makada kicked his legs over Nev's head and brought him back down to the ground. Then he wrapped Nev up between his arms and legs and started to squeeze.

Nev gasped for air. "Holy *sh*—"

"You think I need a *gun* to kill you, you *fuck*?"

Nev saw bright spirals begin to swim before his eyes. He thought of the ways he'd been trained to kill a man in hand-to-hand combat: the top of the head where the joining bones are weak where a powerful hit could cause death, the throat where a chop could squash the windpipe, under the armpit where the slash of a knife could cut through a major artery leading to the heart, the back of a hand where tiny bones are broken easily and could potentially make that hand useless.

Nev knew of these targets and many more, but there weren't any of them he could utilize. Not against Makada. As Makada continued to squeeze, his ears began to ring, and the world began to darken. Unconsciousness looming, Nev wondered if this is what the prey of an Earth python felt like.

Suddenly the fog window got rammed from the outside. A Mauler or Ravager was trying to get in.

Great, Nev thought. Perfect timing. After Makada killed him, one of the beasts could eat him.

"Following me, eh?" Makada said.

He wasn't talking to Nev. He was talking to the Mauler. Nev noticed the SD fire had punched through the glass and weakened it. The glass was ready to shatter, even though it was supposed to be bullet proof. But not against the firepower of an M331a2 weapon system, a.k.a. Shoulder Devil.

Makada had Nev wrapped up. Both of them had hands on the pistol. Makada was intent on turning the pistol toward Nev's head. Nev used up his last bit of strength to make sure that wasn't happening, but he was getting weaker by the second. As they struggled for control over the pistol, its aim moved toward the window the beast was ramming.

Nev yanked the trigger.

The window crashed, the shards toppling inward as a Mauler crawled inside the room, its tail flipping eagerly. Both men scrambled to their feet. The Mauler ignored Nev, completely focused on Makada. It'd been hunting him.

Nev saw anger flash on Makada's face, but he never got the chance to voice it. The Mauler lunged and effortlessly took Makada to the ground, his neck in its jaws.

As Nev ran out of the TOC, he glanced behind him. The Mauler had torn Makada's throat out. Makada was the toughest soldier Nev had ever known, and definitely fought, but he was no match for a Mauler intent on killing him.

Chapter 23

Weapons fire was sparse and sporadic as Nev peeked around the corner of the TOC building. Fort Beckett was mostly moving Maulers and Ravagers. Nev moved slowly, only having a pistol. He didn't have the chance to grab Makada's SD, and besides it was empty. He needed to make it to the barracks or at least start searching for Kate. Hopefully, she wasn't there and already in one of those bunkers—well guarded and safe.

Because he was alone, he knew he could make it. A lone soldier doesn't attract much attention, especially if he knew how to move stealthily. But he wasn't dealing with a normal enemy either. Most likely he'd already been sniffed out, and he wouldn't get much farther without a more powerful weapon. The pistol wouldn't cut it. The only thing it would do is alert more of them to his presence. If he fired it, multiple beasts would eat him as opposed to one. Becoming excrement wasn't on today's task list. Rescuing his wife was. Kate was all that he cared about now. Not the mission. Not the planet. Just her. If he could get to the armory again, he'd have a decent chance. He peeked around the corner of the maintenance building.

Shit.

The few dozen Maulers weren't just surrounding the armory, they were on top of the building, too. Clearly Nev wasn't the only soldier who went for more weapons, and the beasts were on to it. Nev didn't even know if there were any weapons left. He'd been in the stockade for a day. It could be a trap, and the Maulers could be guarding an empty building, making soldiers think there were weapons inside when maybe one of *them* was inside instead.

Best not to think that way, though. It was wise to not underestimate the enemy, but giving them too much credit could hobble the next move. Then again, Nev couldn't help but notice how purposefully they were guarding the armory, like they knew exactly what it was.

Nev inhaled silently, seeing how still the Maulers were. They were waiting for any movement. He *could* move slowly, slow as a shadow so they wouldn't spot him—unless he was upwind. He hoped he wasn't, except he couldn't risk his life needlessly. His death, even though he was willing, might mean Kate's too. That was unacceptable.

Nev wasn't going to fall for the ruse. Those beasts expected their enemy to come to them, which meant Nev had the opportunity to sneak around them. So what if he didn't have a powerful weapon. He'd taken on the Ravagers on his own, except not as many as there now were within the confines of the base. Plus he'd never fought the Maulers before—aside from the one he'd killed inside the stockade—and he didn't know what they were capable of out in the open. Getting to his wife by whatever means necessary was worth the risk of being eaten, but what the next move was after reaching her, he'd yet to decide.

One objective at a time, he thought. Once again what he'd learned in basic training came back to him. He was about to go the opposite direction when a stun grenade blew in front of the armory. The Maulers' hypersensitive hearing made them howl and scatter—at least something other than bullets worked against them, even if it was only temporary.

Nev turned to spot the thrower when he faced a squad of soldiers. They'd come from one of the underground bunkers, the ones Nev had never been in. Four guarded the entrance as another three seemed intent on taking him with them. Before he could thank them, he was hit with a stun gun.

⅄

When Nev came to, he was being dragged. He heard the TOC before he saw it. Another one. Maybe it was established while he was away on Horne's first mission. Probably. He was surprised Horne hadn't come down here himself.

Nev was sat in a chair with his hands zip-tied behind him. Again. Soldiers guarded him, but different from the ones who'd grabbed him from outside. One of them, a medic, dabbed his sore, bloodied face with gauze.

Lieutenant Colonel Mathis approached. He wore his beret. He had short-cropped white hair and studious green eyes. He was sinewy, the way a man his age only could be if he ran almost every day of his military career, probably with a slimmer waistline than most of the young soldiers he commanded.

"Why have I been taken prisoner, sir?"

"For your own protection. You were in the stockade, were you not?"

"For something I didn't do." When Mathis didn't object Nev glanced around the TOC. "What's your mission down here, sir?"

"We are the contingency, but our mission changed once the base was attacked."

"Where are the other soldiers? Are they down here as well?"

"They've been instructed to hang tight as best they can. We're losing. We're plotting a new strategy. I'm sure I don't have to tell you that."

"No, sir. What *was* your mission?"

Mathis almost said but didn't. "It's no longer relevant."

"I want to see my wife."

"Negative. That would mean exposure to the enemy."

"So she's safe?"

"Yes, many are. You'll be reunited once we *all* leave."

Nev smiled. "I always liked you, sir."

"Cut those things off him."

The guard balked. "Sir, he's—"

"Considering what we're dealing with and how well I know Captain Nev, I'm completely unconcerned with what he's suspected of doing."

The guard took out his tactical knife and cut the zip-tie. Nev stood, rubbing his wrists.

"Follow me."

Mathis led Nev into an office and closed the door.

"I never trusted Horne," he said. "Especially after what he'd reported. I knew it was bullshit. Besides, we'll need your help."

"Thank you, sir."

"We lost contact with Colonel Horne before you arrived. As well as Major Makada and Sergeant Major Kayner."

Nev hesitated. "They're gone."

The understanding was unspoken but clear.

"Tell me what happened," Mathis said.

So Nev did, from the beginning, as briefly and with as much detail as he could, considering the battle going on above them. He explained what he went through, the details of the mission, and Horne's treachery. Mathis listened intently and quietly, scarcely taking his eyes off him.

"I believe you, but I'll give Horne this: he believed in what he was doing. He illustrated the importance of my soldiers if he failed. He stayed up top until the end like a captain going down with the ship, even though I implored him to join us. 'What would the men think?' he said."

"I need to know what your mission was, sir. Soldier to soldier."

Mathis exhaled. "Simple. Upon failure of the first wave of soldiers, my battalion has been ordered to advance on the enemy and exterminate them."

"That mission isn't sanctioned by higher. Neither was mine. Horne manipulated those he needed to off-planet, the system altogether. Even the situation reports."

"I had my suspicions."

"We're all expendable, so Horne and those he was in business with can live here. Build their resort or whatever they had planned."

Mathis looked like he'd been gut kicked. "I don't think it's that diabolical, Captain. Did he tell you why he did the things he did?"

"Yes."

"Luxury and basic needs go hand in hand for us humans. I believed in what his intentions were, but there's intent, and then the reality one chooses to accomplish those intentions."

"And facing the reality of any given situation. Horne didn't care about anything but securing this planet. He would have doomed us all."

"If your allegations are accurate, then we have no choice but to abort the mission as it was originally envisioned; however, certain aspects of it must continue if we are to get off this planet alive. As the surviving officer with the highest rank, I'm taking command. Are you prepared to fall under my command, Captain?"

"Yes, sir."

"Do you understand a full investigation will begin once we are off-planet?"

"I hope so, sir."

"Fall in then."

"Yes, sir. I'll need a full briefing."

"You got it."

They went back into the bunker TOC, and Nev was introduced to their intelligence officer.

"This is Lieutenant Brimwald," Mathis said.

"Nice to meet you, sir," Brimwald said.

Nev shook his hand. "Tell me what you know."

"We're taking on the dominant predators of this planet."

"No shit," Nev said. "What about this new one? The Maulers? Where do they fall in with the Ravagers?"

"They could almost be considered Ravagers themselves. Along the lines of an Earth wolf compared to a coyote."

"They're Ravagers too?"

"Closely related. Yes. They dwell on another area of the planet, but somehow they knew there was a threat here. We believe they are fighting alongside the Ravagers."

"We know they are," Mathis said.

"I saw it too," Nev said, "but I also saw them *killing* Ravagers."

"Then those Ravagers must have been outcasts," Brimwald said.

"So which one of them is in charge?" Mathis said.

"Which is in charge between the wolf and the coyote?"

"We aren't talking about wolves and coyotes," Nev said.

"That's the point," Brimwald said. "We don't know. Maybe neither."

Nev grimaced. "I doubt that."

Brimwald grinned. "So do I."

"How could they behave that way?" Mathis said. "They aren't human."

Confusion resounded silently throughout the room.

"In relation to their intelligence they're likely equivalent to humans," Brimwald said, "and we're dealing with a humanlike hierarchy. Maybe even as complicated as our own."

Nev allowed the ramifications of that to sink in. "A complex hierarchy means they definitely have leaders."

"Possibly, but we—"

"The Ravagers do, Lieutenant. I killed one." Nev thought back to the Ravager in the complex as it looked up at him with those intelligent eyes. "How many enemies are there?"

"We don't know. We roughly knew how many were near the…"

"I briefed him," Mathis said.

"Near the dark mountains," Brimwald continued. "But since then they've moved, and our mission has changed."

"What about probes?" Nev said.

"Expended," Mathis said. "Colonel Horne used them all. The ones unaccounted for were assumed to have been destroyed by those flying creatures he described."

"Then we fight to get off this planet with what we've got. What's the plan of action, sir?"

"Horne didn't expend *all* of his arsenal."

"Do we still have specialists that can fire those launchers?"

"I believe so, but we don't know if they're still operational. Considering what the enemy did to the Adelpa aircraft…but Horne had many weapons at his disposal. He didn't let everyone in on them except for myself. He may have been dirty, but he wanted Operation Tuhrelevim to succeed."

Chapter 24

Nev didn't know whether to be ecstatic, like everyone else, or pissed off. He didn't even need to see the aircraft Mathis had put in the air to know what it was, he couldn't, not from where they were. He'd heard it. The unmistakable sound of its powerful engine reverberated throughout the TOC. It was the only one Nev knew of that was still in circulation. Enginsan Adelpa had seen to that.

⅄

The Adelpa 3 fighter jet tearing through the sky overhead caused an effect in more than just the soldiers in the TOC. The beasts reacted as well. All their heads turned up, halting their pursuit so they could inspect the new threat above them.

When the Adelpa 3 fighter cleared the base, it unleashed missiles, engulfing the beasts in flames. The ones hit directly were instantly vaporized. Those at the rim of the blast were thrown off their feet and launched in all directions, and the ones that survived the blast died from the heat wave.

Others were paralyzed. Alive, but not for much longer, moving sluggishly or not at all, the impact from hitting the ground slowly killing them. The beasts that saw the missiles hit, but were unaffected by it, scrambled in whichever direction they could. The base was the last place they wanted to be, their intelligence on hold as instinct kicked in, trying to anticipate where the flying death machine overhead would strike next.

They all looked upward, some moving left and right, stretching their necks to get the best view from their position. The Maulers and Ravagers would do whatever they had to in order to survive. Grouped together they were a larger target, so they had to lessen their ranks, reduce them, which meant splitting up and singles fleeing in all directions.

The Adelpa 3 circled around, its engines echoed its power through the mountains as it throttled gracefully through the sky. It began strafing runs, letting loose with its chain guns, aiming at the beasts near the outer rim of their army, trying to get them to group back together. The Adelpa 3's low-altitude and slow-speed capability allowed precise, near surgical targeting. The funnel of twenty-millimeter bullets shot continuously causing the beasts to inadvertently group together.

The fighter jet ascended fast, nearly straight up, leaned left, and then dove, targeting a large group of the beasts below. And that was when the pilot saw them. "Fire Direction Main, this is Air-Fighter Three-One."

"Go ahead, Three-One," the RTO said.

"Enemy numbers exponentially higher than expected, over."

"Tell me what you see." It was Mathis's voice on the radio. *"How many? Hundreds? Thousands, over?"*

The pilot tilted the stick a fraction to the left, leaning and bulleting over a rolling ocean of predators moving toward Fort Beckett as far back as the mountains in the distance.

"I'd only be guessing, break…Looks close to a million. How copy, over?"

Mathis still held the mic he'd taken from the RTO. "Wilco."

A million.

Nev knew he was right. The Ravagers he'd encountered during his mission were equivalent to one or two soldiers of an entire army. "Where are they headed?"

"Where would you?" Brimwald said.

"But that many isn't showing up on our scanners—" a soldier said.

"Could they have changed their body temperature?" Nev said.

"That's not possible," Mathis said sternly, holding up the mic. "That would mean they understand—"

"I wouldn't put *understanding* past them," Nev said.

Mathis raised the mic. "Air-Fighter Three-One, Fire Direction Main."

"This is Air-Fighter Three-One, over."

"Roger, Air-Fighter Three-One, concentrate all fire at base, break... Upon expenditure of all munitions, standby to land for rearmament, over."

"Wilco."

⅄

The Adelpa 3 pulled a hard left and flattened out, its engine thundering far behind it, soaring through the sky like an Earth hawk that never flapped its wings. The pilot chose targets surrounding the base, the singles and small groups at the borders. It fired its chain guns, killing as many as possible until it fired its remaining missiles.

Tuhrelevim was once again on fire, the beasts being blasted to death in a beautifully hot, crimson fireball with a rumble that extinguished the anger, howls, and roars of those that it killed. The residue from the explosions hung in the air, as a deadly, toxic gas.

The beasts that weren't killed by the missiles breathed that gas into their lungs. They coughed and gagged; some vomited, struggled to breathe, and collapsed. The toxin either killed them or incapacitated them. Most didn't live long.

"Fire Direction Main, munitions expended, over."

"Roger, Air-Fighter Three-One. Return to base for refueling and rearmament, over."

"Wilco. Approaching."

The aircraft had done significant damage, but there were so many Ravagers and Maulers that further strafes were necessary. Nev had joined the security platoon at ground level, guarding the runway where the Adelpa 3 would land. The assault on the beasts had ensured the jet's ingress had been cleared. At least temporarily, hopefully long enough to rearm and refuel.

Under heavy guard, the boots and the soldiers who wore them were spread and ready, assuming attack formations, ready to blow away anything that showed teeth. They needed that aircraft to be airborne again and fast, so it could resume death from above.

From the top of a cliff, a Ravager gained speed. Long claws embedded in the dirt with each planted step, and hard gallops drove it. The other Ravagers cleared the way as it accelerated, gallop after gallop. Then it propelled its large frame straight off the cliff and into the air.

It turned, snarled, and was hit by the Adelpa 3 fighter jet. The Ravager was obliterated, crushed into red spray and blood and bits of flesh and bone. The nose of the jet crushed inward, its trajectory thrown off, and it lost altitude quickly.

Nev and the others watched in horror as the Adelpa 3 spun, rocketed overhead with a deafening, out of control whine over them, and crashed just outside Fort Beckett. Tuhrelevim rocked from the blast, the smoke and fire instantly rising within view.

The beasts roared in the distance, well aware of the victory. The barks and snarls seemed to be coming from everywhere at once. Above, beyond, and somehow it even sounded like they were coming from below, there were so many. The soldiers were reminded how surrounded they were.

The pilot no doubt felt lucky he'd been able to eject initially, but probably wished he'd been in the jet when it crashed. As he floated toward the ground, his chute moving across the sky as light as a feather, a dozen Ravagers looked up, following at a pace as slow as the parachute was taking him through the sky. When the pilot got close to the ground, he screamed right before he was tackled midair.

Nev and the others pointlessly fired their weapons from a distance.

"What the hell are we going to do now?" Mathis asked rhetorically.

The TOC was silent. The men did their best to get their bearings, all of them quickly deducing the results of the mission and mentally rebooting.

"Can we warn off the pop-ship?" Mathis said.

The RTO shook his head. "Negative, sir."

"Why not?"

"Tuhrelevim's atmosphere," he said. "Choppy comms. They're too far out."

"But once they get closer."

"By then they'll have no choice but to land. Gravity on this planet, sir. They must land before they can take off again."

"Damn it." He grabbed a mic. "Captain Nev, what's your location?"

"Incoming, sir!"

"The most intelligent predators on Tuhrelevim are converging on our location," Mathis said. "We've invaded their world, and they're very aware of us trying to take their home away from them. I have no doubt that if we stay here any longer we'll eventually fight the entire planet. What about the pop-ships behind the first?"

"They're spaced out enough so that they'll rely on the first landing safely," Brimwald said.

"Which isn't going to happen," Mathis said.

"The others must be contacted and briefed by the first ship before landing. They'll relay the sit-rep. They'll be turned away."

Nev appeared on the run with the other soldiers behind. "Got a plan, sir. Before I knew about the Adelpa three—"

"Just tell me what you need, Captain."

Chapter 25

The Adelpa 4 loomed in the sky like a dark, pill-shaped cloud. Many of the beasts took notice too, staring upward. If it were to land on the runway now, before its descent path could be cleared by the soldiers on the ground, everyone on board would be killed. The beasts wouldn't stop until they'd hunted down each and every human being. Every second counted.

Better for those on board that they couldn't see out. It would only be unending viciousness and teeth and claws hoping to sink into them. Most of the families on board were probably still asleep. Hopefully they'd only have nightmares of the terrors that awaited them and never have to face the real thing, unless the soldiers failed.

The skiffs were tagged. Mathis would be able to locate them on the scanners, allowing him to pinpoint their location from the TOC in case they needed reinforcements. Not that it would do them any good. Outnumbered wasn't an apt-enough description of their situation. They'd all be dead before any reinforcements could arrive. Captain Nev and the soldiers on the skiff mission were on their own.

Skiffs had been on standby since the original Ravager attacks, after the civilian explorers didn't return, and including the one Nev had discovered on his way back to Fort Beckett, that made three skiffs speeding toward the enemy. Each one was weighted down with automated ammo boxes. Excluding the driver, all soldiers on the mission were armed with two Shoulder Devils each. Kill shots were hoped for but not expected. Maiming was the secondary objective. There wasn't a third. Their mission was to reduce enemy numbers any way possible. Period.

The soldiers considered their sector of fire to be the side of the skiff they faced. Nev and another soldier were on the lead skiff covering twelve o'clock, the other two skiffs were at three o'clock and nine o'clock. With at least one of the SD operators aiming off the rear of the three o'clock and nine o'clock skiffs, it gave them a full clock of control.

Though there were mostly Ravagers, Maulers were intermingled. The two species seemed to be separated into squads and even platoons. The roar of them was deafening, even over the skiff engines.

As the driver steered at top speed, Nev covered twelve o'clock. His SDs ascended quickly, whined their three-second delay, and fired, hitting the enemy deep in their front rank. They dispersed just enough.

"Now!"

The others fired a wall of lead, Shoulder Devils dropping Ravagers and Maulers in their wake, chewing up the beasts before them and carving a bloody path across the field for the skiffs to plow through at one hundred miles per hour.

Communication between the soldiers was minimal. They'd planned it that way, expecting what rampaged toward them. Once the tip of the beast army dispersed enough for the soldiers to get through, each skiff realigned and moved to their designated positions, aiming at their predetermined sectors of fire. With all six shooters holding two SDs each and all twelve SDs firing at the same time—four up front, two on either side of the other skiffs, and two aiming at the rear—they maintained their assault as a clock with every hour covered. Fortunately for the humans, most of the enemy was heading south toward Fort Beckett, which meant they could still make it back—as long as their mission was remotely successful.

Decreasing enemy numbers ensured a safer landing for the Adelpa 4 once it arrived. Then the beasts prowling the base would be targeted, instead of focusing on the astronomical number of them rampaging toward it. The soldiers that handled the SDs were the best at Fort Beckett that were still alive.

That included Nev. He had the most experience firing SDs of any of them, now that Makada was dead.

Nev targeted Ravagers and Maulers alike, the powerful weapons chewing up their flesh as the skiffs drove across the high green grass at one hundred miles per hour. The beasts couldn't keep up with the vehicles, so they tried to lead the skiffs and leap on them as they passed, but Nev's twelve o'clock firing position took care of those.

Nev activated his shoulder radio. "Stay away from the cliffs!"

The nine o'clock skiff steered right, closing the gap to the group. They weren't going to allow a Ravager to take out a skiff the same way they'd taken out the Adelpa aircraft if they could help it.

The skiffs were doing damage. Not to their numbers overall, the beasts had far too many, but within the sector they'd prioritized. They knew it too. They barked and snarled and swiped in frustration as the skiffs passed them.

The SDs constant firing sounded like a continuous, drawn-out explosion as both species fought over the beautiful world. Tall, craggy, snow-tipped mountains surrounded them, watching like patient spectators unwilling to choose sides.

"There's something going on at the center," Nev said. "You see how their ranks stay deep and face us?"

"Yes, sir," the driver said.

The Ravager army swirled like they were protecting something that didn't decrease in depth until it suddenly did.

Holy shit.

"That one in the middle," Nev said. "See him?"

The largest Ravager anyone had ever seen appeared, like a general behind his swirling army, its massive face dwarfing the guards that protected it, like a queen bee compared to her drones. Its lips drew back in a confident sneer, nearly a smile, with teeth the size of a man's arm. It had a brindled pattern like the leader Nev had killed in the complex, mostly dark with white stripes—the reverse of the other Ravagers. Ravagers had been protecting it, but now it looked exposed, as if it wasn't supposed to be, not unlike Horne before Nev shot him.

The skiff drove around the undulating mass of running beasts. Even though the one Nev thought of as the general was out in the open, there were still many Ravagers guarding it. Take it out, and they'd have a better chance, even if he wasn't the only one. An army without a leader—even temporarily—was weaker and more vulnerable.

"Concentrate all fire on him!" Nev shouted.

The skiffs opened fire, pelting the Ravagers and Maulers, and they surged full force. Then the General left the group that protected it behind. They galloped hard to try to keep up but couldn't. The General was too fast. Ravagers leaped in front of the SDs line of fire, sacrificing themselves as Nev and his men tried to take out their commander.

The humans and beasts battled at high speed. The skiffs kept their distance the best they could, the SDs a constant rumble of gunfire until one soldier on the nine o'clock skiff had to reload. The Ravagers went after the skiff itself, lunging and bumping, growling and roaring, trying to climb on and take advantage of the humans' momentary setback.

Most were shot off before they could get a grip, but then one Mauler, using a shot Ravager as a shield, climbed over it, and before anyone could do anything, took a massive swipe at the driver. It clawed his neck and left shoulder horribly, almost tearing his head off. Blood erupted, and he slumped over, dead.

The nine o'clock skiff drifted even farther toward its position of time. One of the soldiers threw down his SD controllers, the SDs themselves crashing in the dirt, and shoved the dead driver out of the way to take over the controls, but it was too late. The entire skiff got swallowed up by bloodthirsty animals.

The control of the battle shifted, and the Ravager General bounded forward, keeping up with the skiffs, and swiped with a massive paw, crushing the front half of the three o'clock skiff. Its trajectory was stopped so suddenly that the soldiers flew over the top of it. One was crushed by the skiff when it landed. The others were torn apart within seconds. No screams were heard, not over the growls of the Ravagers and the Maulers that fell upon them, shredded by the endless flood of jaws and claws.

Then the General looked directly at Nev, watching as the twelve o'clock skiff drove past the endless waves of beasts, now completely focused on him. Leaders sometimes recognized one another.

They wouldn't be able to get to the General. It had suddenly become too well guarded. The remaining skiff veered off, and Nev kept his balance, aimed, and fired thousands of rounds in its direction anyway. Both SDs clicked empty, and Nev docked them to reload.

With the other skiffs destroyed, all of the Ravagers and Maulers were coming after them now. Because they'd driven past so many and created such a large path to go through, without the other skiffs their ingress had closed. All of the beasts they'd passed were now ahead of them as they tried to get back to base. And they didn't have the firepower they'd had on the way out.

The reloaded SDs hovered over Nev's shoulders once again, and he changed his sector of fire to the rear. The other soldier fired from the front corners. The gap they'd created was closing fast. They were about to get swallowed up like the other skiffs had. Nev thought of Kate, aimed both SDs, and fired for the last time.

Ravagers suddenly swarmed the General, leaping on top and engulfing it and then one another, burying their leader, making it unreachable. It was curious that they thought Nev was such a threat, piling on top of it the way they did, but Nev continued to fire into them anyway, hoping there was a slim chance the General would show its face again. At least Nev knew he would kill many of them before his own death.

Then Nev heard a familiar whistle, and the large pile of Ravagers that were protecting their leader exploded into fire. To the left of the skiff was another explosion, giving the Ravagers in pursuit pause. They scrambled away before another impact, and then another. The beasts were being annihilated.

The launchers!

⅄

"Fire mission!" Mathis stood in front of a digital topographical map, eyeing the skiffs as they moved across it. "Danger close! Coordinates four eight six two eight three...nine eight two nine nine."

"Roger, sir," the RTO said. He pressed the mic. "Attention all launchers, this is Fire Direction Main. Fire mission, danger close, coordinates—"

⅄

There were six launchers in all, spaced out on steel spin wheels used to load and off-load them from transport ships. They were belted down, steady and unreachable by the frustrated Ravagers and Maulers that stalked below them.

The Adelpa launchers raised their azimuths, ensuring different target areas, fully capable of destroying any of the grid squares that Mathis so meticulously studied if he commanded it. The launchers only rocked slightly as they fired their ordnance. The rocket back-blast exploded toxic smoke across the terrain, and the multiple launch shot through the sky.

The whistle of the rockets whined before the steel rain broke apart, dividing into many munitions as opposed to one. Powerful on their own, together they obliterated the ground, hitting moving targets they honed in on, their impact and concussions rocking Tuhrelevim and blasting deep holes wherever they missed one of the beasts. The land was suddenly engulfed in flame, and the beasts in range of the rocket attack struggled to live through the fire.

The ordnance charred the ground, changing the landscape for years to come. Nothing would grow there long after.

Mathis's explosive cover barrage had created substantial distance between the beasts and the skiff as planned. The other soldier now aimed his SDs behind the skiff and fired as Nev covered the front, firing at any of the beasts that weren't intimidated by the rocket attack, the ones that got too close, all the while hoping they'd make it back on time.

Even with the devastation of steel rain, the Maulers and Ravagers were still galloping after them. Nev couldn't see the General. Hopefully it was dead.

Chapter 26

The size of the Adelpa 4 got larger as they approached. They were reminiscent of the old aircraft carriers on Earth, but with no visible flight deck or bridge. All of that was structured internally now. It hadn't landed on the runway. It couldn't. There were too many beasts waiting for it, as if they knew where it intended to land. Instead it was forced to land on the unsteady terrain just outside the base. The skiff mission had disrupted the enemy enough so they could at least do that.

They could hear weapons fire and the constant roar of the beasts battling to get to the pop-ship. Nev and the others on the skiff would have joined the defense from afar, but they'd expended the rest of their ammo even before Fort Beckett had been in sight. Instead they slowed, creating a barrier against a building, giving them enough time to join the soldiers protecting the families.

Their SDs were out of ammo, but Fort Beckett still had Rovla assault rifles and plenty of ammo for them. On their own, the smaller caliber weapons might take out one Ravager or Mauler before it took you down, but with a squad or entire platoon firing them at once, the line of fire was nearly impenetrable.

Unless their enemies were willing to sacrifice themselves—which was exactly what they were prepared to do, and doing, barreling into the human defenses as their families made their way to the Adelpa 4, trying to get at them, clearly understanding their importance. The soldiers had fought as ordered up until now, but with their loved ones at risk, they fired at will, even breaking ranks. One soldier jumped onto a Mauler about to swipe at a nearby woman. The beasts weren't the only ones that could sacrifice themselves.

Grenades exploded, launching guts and body parts and blood. Nev didn't see Kate as the continuous onslaught of beasts poured over Fort Beckett. He caught glimpses of Ravagers like the leader he'd killed in the complex, different from the others with their white stripes and size. Though nowhere near as big as the General, they were also leaders, and Nev wondered if they were the General's direct offspring.

Mathis was yelling at his shoulder radio. He must have been communicating to the captain of the Adelpa 4, because its defense system activated. Two massive turret cannons lowered and fired, cranking out rounds in a powerful, continuous flash blast of projectiles. Their operators from the internal bridge actually shot at the beasts around the people. They were that accurate.

Because the cannons were functional, they should have been firing already, and that was probably why Mathis was still red-faced and yelling into his radio, chewing out whoever was in charge on that ship. With the Adelpa 4 security cannons active, Nev waved his arm, trying his best to communicate to the soldiers to break formation and board. Then he saw her.

"Kate!"

She turned and said something Nev couldn't hear. Nev threw an arm around her, and they ran as the battle continued around them. They didn't have time to say anything to each other, nor could they, not with the weapons fire and snarling and roaring of the vicious beasts. Nev would get her on board and then rejoin the battle.

A panic erupted as the Ravagers were able to get to one of the cannons. They bombarded the cannon from the sides, hanging, ripping, and clawing at it until it was bent, sparks flying, rounds stutter-firing, and then the high shriek of tearing metal as it was—impossibly—wrenched loose.

Almost everyone ran except for Mathis and a platoon of soldiers. When Nev stopped alongside him, pointing for Kate to continue on board, Mathis grabbed Nev by his collar. "Protect the people in case they get in! Get on board with your wife! That's an order!"

Then he threw Nev toward the ramp and continued to wave everyone past him, still yelling into his radio. If he'd been alone, Nev would have stayed with him, no matter what he'd ordered him to do, but he had to think of Kate. Only her safety mattered to him now.

They hurried inside among the families that were already on board, and those who hadn't set foot off the ship. In a way Nev envied them. They'd never see Tuhrelevim, never feel that tug of wanting it and the disappointment that it would never be their home.

The Adelpa 4's powerful engines coughed to full power, ready to take off again.

Nev turned Kate to face him. They'd been together long enough to read each other's lips, necessary considering how loud the Adelpa 4's engines were. "You OK?" he mouthed.

Kate nodded shakily. "Are you?" she mouthed back.

Something crashed near the entrance, and Kate went wide-eyed. Soldiers were fighting, and mouths and claws were rising up and trying to get in, trying to get at the people on board.

Nev guided Kate to a seat as he and the other soldiers aimed their Rovlas, ready to fire. One rapid-fired a mine layer as far out of the Adelpa 4 as he could. The disk-shaped motion sensing weapons exploded on impact, consistently landing in the midst of the rampaging beasts. Miniature blood volcanoes erupted.

The other security cannon still fired and knocked out chunks of the beast wall behind Mathis. Then it sputtered and must have been destroyed, too, because it no longer shot. Then the wall of Ravagers and Maulers rose up again, surging.

There was screaming, the way men sound when they're being torn apart. Mathis was still yelling something Nev couldn't hear, to the other soldiers fighting by his side. Mathis firing his Rovla was the last thing Nev saw before the ramp closed.

The Adelpa 4 creaked and groaned as it lifted off. The surface of Tuhrelevim and all its chaos blocked out finally, the people inside the ascending aircraft could now hear one another speak. Not that they needed to. What Nev saw in Kate's eyes let him know that she'd seen things he wished she never had. Things that would stay with her for the rest of her life.

Chapter 27

Nev had been in the military mind-set for so long, since he'd left for the complex, it was a relief to finally turn it off and let someone else be in charge. The responsibility had collapsed in his mind as if it he'd been holding a hundred pounds over his head and was finally able to let it drop. He hadn't even asked where they were going. It didn't matter. *Away* was all that did. No doubt they would be briefed soon about their next steps. After docking at one of the many transfer stations, Nev and Kate would decide where to go from there. Nev planned to turn in his retirement request. If he was denied, he didn't care. He was done with the military.

He glanced around and saw vacant, wide eyes of the family members who'd boarded. The rest of the population was on the upper levels. He didn't even know how many people were on board. He hadn't memorized that information, his mind deeming it useless, as if he always knew deep down they weren't staying.

No one said much. What was said could only be heard by the person they were saying it to. Hushed, weak voices. Everyone just wanted to get as far away from the planet as possible. What had happened on Tuhrelevim would most likely be described—to those who had a vested interest—as a severe storm and its aftermath, the only question being whether it would be worth their time and money to clean it up. Whether *they* still deemed it inhabitable, Nev could only guess, but in his opinion, that world would never be occupied by humans. It belonged to its beasts.

Nev forcibly dismissed his feelings of frustration. He had to. They were already eating him up inside. There'd be plenty of time for him to mentally go over everything that had happened later. Even though Kate was sleeping, she clutched at Nev as she dreamed. She must have been exhausted. Even under the tumultuous circumstances, it felt incredible to be near her.

When she and Nev had been reunited—even though in hindsight he knew there'd been no time and it would be ridiculous with everything that was going on around them—he'd wanted to see a smile or a sign of relief showing she was glad he was still alive, but there'd been nothing like that. Just an expression of terror. He couldn't get her face out of his mind, like he'd been looking at someone else and not his wife.

Turbulence shook the Adelpa 4 and Kate's eyes popped open. She let out a whimper, trying to escape her seatbelt, gasping for breath.

"You're OK," Nev said soothingly, holding her. "You're safe."

Even as he forced out the comforting words, Nev could tell they'd had little effect. Kate was severely traumatized by what she'd seen. What she'd been through. Nev felt so sorry for allowing that to happen, for being stationed here, for bringing her here. The other passengers watched blankly as Nev tried to calm his hysterical wife.

He gently grasped her wrists, trying to get her to stay seated. She had blood on her. Nev realized his focus had only been her eyes so far—her beautiful, terrified eyes. There were specks of blood on her cheek and throat, and there were clumps of that and something else in her hair. It wasn't hers, though; she didn't have any wounds, so it must have been someone else's.

"Let go of me!"

"You're safe. Try to relax, please. I've got you."

She stopped struggling and was suddenly still. Thinking back. "The things they did to the people—"

"I tried to get back sooner. I'm sorry I wasn't able to."

"Those things they—"

Kate was trembling, starting to fidget.

"I love you," he said.

She tried to stand, once again forgetting she was belted in, forcing herself against her husband's grip.

"They're…*out there*!" she screamed.

It pained him so much to see her like this. Nev wanted to take her trauma away, have all of it go in to him, somehow, so she wouldn't have to bear it, but he knew that wasn't possible. All he could do was allow tears to roll down his cheeks and hold her close.

Chapter 28

A Mauler climbed high, to the top of a smoldering building, looking out, scanning. All of Fort Beckett smoked, as if showing all of Tuhrelevim who had won the war. Beasts moved about freely below, as if the base had been theirs to begin with. The soldiers who'd ensured the people would escape onto the Adelpa 4 were all dead now, but that didn't stop the Maulers from nosing through the rubble, hunting for more of them to kill.

Farther away, where the skiff battle had taken place, a group of wounded Ravagers stood together, scarred from the human artillery weapons. They were larger than most that surrounded them. They stared ahead with discipline and didn't flinch as Maulers approached them, raising their jaws up to reach the tough skin under their necks. They sank their teeth into the Ravagers' throats, yanking down and ripping until blood poured.

The General, blackened, scarred, and bloody, looked on. Severe burns marked the side of its face, leading up to where one of its eyes had been burned out of its socket. A few Ravager females licked at the wet, charred chunks that dribbled down its cheek. The females were of equal height but slimmer than their more muscular male counterparts.

The General stood up, dwarfing them as it did, and shook them away, looking nearly as tall as a giant over those it ruled. It wasn't proud that the Ravagers it had chosen to lead its army had failed, but it respected them for accepting their fate.

The Ravager leaders fell to the ground as they bled to death. The Maulers responsible, bloody faced, disappeared within the ranks of the hundreds of thousands surrounding them, silent as they watched.

The General looked over to another group of Ravagers with its remaining eye. There were just as many of them, the same size or bigger than those that had just been executed. These were the ones it had chosen to take their place.

C.A. Gleason was born in Seattle in 1976. He graduated from the Los Angeles Film School with a major in directing. Following a three-year enlistment in the military, he began turning his short film and movie ideas into cinematic fiction. He lives in the Pacific Northwest, where he creates tales of action, horror, science fiction, mystery, and fantasy.

www.ingramcontent.com/pod-product-compliance
Lightning Source LLC
LaVergne TN
LVHW010110170826
845678LV00012B/2324

* 9 7 8 1 9 8 4 1 9 3 0 9 4 *